Bars of America

Bars of America

Neil Ferguson

Hamish Hamilton : London

First published in Great Britain 1986
by Hamish Hamilton Ltd
Garden House 57–59 Long Acre London WC2E 9JZ

British Library Cataloguing in Publication Data

Ferguson, Neil
   Bars of America.
   I. Title
   813′.54[F]   PS3556.E71/

ISBN 0–241–11875–1

Typeset at The Spartan Press Ltd,
Lymington, Hants
Printed in Great Britain by
St Edmundsbury Press, Bury St Edmunds, Suffolk

For
Sarah

Contents

Limies

In the summer of nineteen seventy-six the aging luxury liner, *SS Caronia*, running before a typhoon in the South China Sea, struck reefs and went down with the good timing that the well-bred always display in the face of adversity. The era of luxury liners was over. Within a few years the *Caronia* – 715 feet, 34,000 tons and known to her admirers as the Green Goddess – would have been towed to the breakers' yard anyway. Her pre-War elegance was out of fashion. How many souls were lost is not recorded, but one thing we know is that the ship's bar was a spacious corridor running crossbows, like many ship's bars, so that in stormy weather the pitch would be back-and-forth rather than the side-to-side yaw most frequenters of bars are already familiar with. We know that the bar-counter was a piece of mahogany with a carved diadem bulge in the centre of it, a feminine touch that kept the place from looking like a Hangtown saloon and subtly allowed passengers to converse across it without necessarily having to drink with each other. The décor of the bar was in a style that has not been in *Vogue* since the Third Republic. Plate mirror-glass behind the bottles behind the barman allowed the drinkers to keep an eye on themselves – there is no more sobering sight than of oneself getting drunk – although the small quantity of light leaking from the portal wall-lamps made sure that no one was going to be observed too intimately. It was all done in a style which these days we find repro'ed in almost every High Street fern bar and up-market discotheque: Astaire ritz. The style is back in fashion. But if it's the real thing you're looking for, take a walk along 8th Street to where Fifth Avenue begins and poke your nose into the bar of the good ship *Caronia*, lovingly extracted from her sunken hulk, restored and carrying the name One Fifth – as stylish a bar as you could want to get wrecked in.

In the One Fifth, on the bar-stool next to me, Geoff Morse said: '. . . on the rocks.'

Having taken our order and placed in front of both of us a paper napkin with the monogram of the bar on it, the barman set about fixing our drinks, his hand reaching in among his top shelf for the bottle of Tanqueray with a precision that had taken years of daily practice: Schnabel picking out a poignant minor chord in a tricky arpeggio, and like him he wore a starched white shirt, black bow-tie and the unsmiling expression of the great artist capable of touching the heart. He was a tall good-looking young man with unfashionable wavy red-dish-brown hair and a parting in it that made him look like an Ivy League college graduate, one who had studied Law and hated it, played a bit of football, a character in a story by Scott Fitzgerald. He probably had a girl somewhere who owned a gun which she kept after him to get some bullets for, to shoot him with when he did. He placed two drinks on the napkins and took one of the five-dollar bills from the bar without saying a word. All you could hear was the sound of ice cracking and, at the sink, a Philippino bar-boy polishing glasses, looking at nothing. He probably had a girl somewhere too.

Geoff Morse had not been explaining the way he wanted the drinks – the barman already knew that – or even the last hours of the *SS Caronia*; it was the state of his marriage he had been referring to. When the drinks arrived he let the subject drop, not only to spare the barman the details of his personal life but in deference to the two drinks: dry Tanqueray gin and Rose's Lime Cordial in just proportion, pale in thin tumblers with little straws to swizzle with. Level on the bar like a pair of scales, balanced, they had that equality about them which

4

every friendship aspires to. Next to that, what was a broken marriage?

We were drinking gimlets, partly because they beat martinis hollow and partly because we always did when we visited this particular bar, which we tried to do at the same hour, between afternoon and evening. Until the office workers arrived we would be the only customers and the Philippino bar-boy had time to dream about his girl in the Philippines. And, too, because this was my last night in New York. We were saying goodbye to each other. Again. Over gimlets you always seem to be. There's something about that cocktail, perhaps the dry taste it leaves in the mouth, that possesses the essential properties of poignant occasions. In its presence, friendship alone just doesn't seem enough.

Sweating, we watched the drinks for a while, abashed, like a pair of schoolboys eyeing two girls across a dance-floor before taking the plunge. Our sweat cooled. It may have been late afternoon and temperate where we were sitting but outside the digital weather-gauges on top of the Wall Street financial institutions were registering up in the eighties. It had been one of those days even New Yorkers call warm. This morning, like every other recently, the man from the FM radio station who announced the Weather Report in the same voice he did the advertisements for the air-conditioning company repeated the forecast of a 30% likelihood of precipitation – in other words it might rain but then it might not. The percentage always remained constant but the humidity level rose steadily with every bulletin like share prices before a crash. It was like waiting for the outbreak of war; something cataclysmic was going to happen soon, but for the time being there wasn't a cloud in the sky. Perfect weather for an assassination.

The barman drifted by and asked how our drinks were. We told him they were fine and he continued on his way.

Geoff Morse said: 'When I first came over here – before I met up with Alice – I had no idea what I was doing here, why I had come. I just kicked around California with the coke crowd until I landed the rigger's job in Sausalito . . . .'

When Geoff first came over here – a decade ago now – I had packed a half-bottle of Gordon's in his grip in case he needed one, like the explorer's mum packing his *polenta*. I drove him

5

to the airport – in silence because I was meant to be going with him – and we drank the other half neat without ice out of disposable plastic beakers in the deserted cafeteria while immigrant workers swept around us. The warm gin tasted awful, which was just how we felt, which makes it one of the memorable cocktails, possessing the essential properties of its occasion. We christened it 'The Heathrow' – if you don't have raw grain spirit, you could always try disinfectant – because watching someone disappear through the final gates into the departure lounge of an international airport *is* awful; there is no ceremony to it, no detail for the imagination to get to grips with. Voyagers are not carried off by the wheels of circumstance, disappearing into the distance by slow degrees, but seem to step freely out of your life. They might as well be stepping into a public toilet. Only you know they are not.

'. . . at the time all I wanted to do was get the hell out of England. I couldn't breathe there. But neither did I understand what America was about. I was too correct, too English. I wouldn't even cruise a red light.'

'But,' I said, 'you sat next to Alice while *she* did.'

'Let's say I began to cut a few corners.'

'Until you ended up driving around on stolen credit cards.'

Geoff shrugged. My disapproval was the least of his worries. In affairs of the heart you begin by making every sacrifice. In Geoff's case, for love of Alice, it had been his integrity.

'*You* know Alice. With her that was normal. She wouldn't call it stealing. It was just how she was raised. As a kid she was given everything she needed, so as an adult she took anything she wanted. All her family and neighbours are the same. Most people she ever knew are into shady deals. Her father is a New York cop, a law enforcement officer, and he's been taking kick-backs all his life, a TV here, a camera there. He doesn't think about it. Why should he? No one else does.'

Geoff Morse raised his glass and sipped the medicine, the age-old prescription for the ailment he was suffering from.

'*I* was the one out of sync. Alice made stealing and lying into an exciting game. There was even a kind of frankness in the way she went about it after the nice scruples you and I were brought up to observe. For a time I was under her spell.'

He didn't have to tell me. As best man at their wedding –

which had taken place in Egypt, in the presence of Horus – I had seen it all and I wanted to slap him, but by the time I arrived on the scene it was already too late. I couldn't dissuade them from riding the railways without paying, which Alice, of course, found a way to do. Geoff loves steam trains, we both do, and out there travelling on them costs next to nothing. In no time we found ourselves lying to honest railwaymen. In Cairo I watched Geoff and Alice report to the Tourist Police the loss of a thousand dollars in American Express cheques which were still in their pockets. A month later they went back to the same police station to report them lost a second time. What chance did semi-literate Egyptian policemen have against New York street hustle? That was my first sight of Alice at work, a smooth-talking sexy blonde dope queen among the gentle-mannered Moslems.

'Oh sure,' Geoff said. 'She never wants to pay for her ticket if she can get a free ride. That's how she goes through life. She's smart. Has to make a dupe of everyone. She can't help it. She steals from the store even though I give her plenty of money.'

'And she persuaded you to steal,' I said. Like a good friend I wasn't going to spare his feelings.

'Like I said, she doesn't think of it as stealing. For a while neither did I. Here, parents give their children whatever they want: toys, money, food, anything except rules for right and wrong. When they grow up their parents are mildly surprised because their children lie to them, steal from the store, have drug problems. They can't think where they went wrong. How can you blame the kids? They were never taught to value a thing. They treat everything they own as if it were junk. If it breaks, they can always get hold of a replacement. And it goes without saying, what other people own has no value either. To the kids of Queens and Brooklyn it's all junk – the cars, the trains, the City itself. It will probably be true of my own kids.'

New York. Junk City. But except for the packaging – Woody Allen's Manhattan – you get the feeling it isn't really a city at all, in the usual sense, but a conurbation of ghettos of emigrants who got off the boat and stayed put. 'I love NY', sweatshirts brag, but not to the extent of paying for the maintenance of the place. Most of the housing is falling into

7

the street, the streets are cracked and pitted and full of heaps that were once beautiful cars, trash that hasn't been collected, debris, broken glass. One reason New Yorkers love Mayor Koch is because he's tough on the unions. The skyline of Queens – where Geoff lived – was one of derelict baroque factories, empty shells, idle derricks on rusting gantries, water towers, cemeteries, crumbling overhead subway trains linking beat-up stations with names like Euclid Avenue and Ozone Park, the beat-up trains patroled by young black youths in green berets to keep the passengers from getting beat-up also. An exhausted undercapitalized landscape that still, nevertheless, has its charm.

'Alice can't tell any more what she has a right to and what she hasn't. And that's what I can't take anymore: the *imprecision*! No one cares! People bend the rules how they want – language, traffic regulations, ethics. In this town you make your own rules. Nobody blames the President when he gets his hands caught in the till. You heard Alice's sister explaining to her why she didn't want to put down on the Medicaid Insurance form the fact that the baby was pre-mature, in case that counted against him in some future claim. It probably won't. It's just a matter of course to manipulate the facts for reasons of expediency.'

'She wouldn't call that a lie,' I said. 'But you two never could agree on what anything is called.'

In a jokey way nomenclature was a long-standing conten-tious subject between Geoff and Alice. Sometimes they didn't speak the same language.

'Oh sure. She's only lying from our point of view. You and I tell lies like anyone else but we know when we are and feel bad when we do. People like Alice don't feel anything; they don't even know they *are* telling lies. To them there are valid and non-valid versions of the truth and you have to be *smart* to know the difference. Why do you think they elected a crooked lawyer and a Hollywood actor to run their business, people who are professionals at giving fiction the appearance of fact? That's what I mean by imprecision.'

The barman tossed a glance in our direction, then took away the glasses and passed them, without speaking, to the Philippino who immediately washed them. Between the handsome cocktail barman and the foreign bar-boy was a gulf of race and class no conversation could bridge. Into fresh glasses he poured freely from the bottle a measure which he knew was to our taste. No imprecision there – 'hand and eye', as they teach you in figure-drawing classes in Art School. He took five bills from Geoff's pile, counting them silently in front of us. 'Have one yourself,' Geoff told him.

The barman nodded and helped himself to a bottle of Molson from the fridge.

'. . . John De Lorean says he makes cars when he's dealing coke. Alice tells the children I'm at work when I'm upstairs taking a nap – what the hell? It's easier than explaining the truth because they'd only come up and wake me. Well, that's valid in the circumstances. What she's doing is teaching a three-year-old the same thing she was taught – to accept an easy lie instead of an unpalatable truth.'

'It may be just a question of nomenclature.' I said.

All the kids on the block, including Geoff's, I had noticed, called insects 'bugs', which were usually found in the 'dirt'. I realized that these words were standard American but I hadn't realized that they connoted attitudes of loathing. It didn't matter what kind of insects were being discussed – ants, beetles, caterpillars – they were all bugs; they were dirty, foreign bodies. The kids and Alice talked about them with the cheerful alienation of B52 bomber pilots. The backyard was a South-east Asian landscape seen from a great height. The insects had no names and the children no means of distinguishing a bee from a yellowjacket, the harmless from the dangerous, the good from the bad.

'Alice hates it when we get the dictionaries out and argue over what words mean. And maybe she has a point. It's our obsession to think it matters. I don't care that Alice's friends don't know where Australia is, just that they aren't interested. It isn't a useful piece of information. Regan's top advisor on foreign policy was a Supreme Court Judge who failed his Law exams; when Congress vetted him he didn't know the names of the capitals of half the South American countries. They gave him the job anyway . . . .'

To Geoff, because he wasn't American, America wasn't an idea; it was just a place like any other and he could only talk about it through the narrow frame of his experiences, his wife, his observations. At heart he was English, because he was an empiricist. But he had no time for that snotty attitude of Europeans towards the place, especially the English – who giggle at the checkered trousers American tourists wear and the way they pronounce 'Birmingham'. That was just what he liked about the place. He owned a pair of plaid shorts himself which he wore when he came back from work and cooked hamburgers on the barbecue in the backyard for his kids and the neighbours' kids. He had learnt to flatten his English vowels and make the soft alveolar 't'; like everyone else in New York he had almost eliminated the perfect aspect from his concept of Time: 'Say, did you get the beers yet?' Someone from Blighty would know him for what he was eventually, but most Americans would probably take him for one of themselves. And in many ways they wouldn't have been wrong. He drove a beat-up Cadillac to work and traded gags with the neighbours over the fence. Except that he read the William Safire column in the *Times* on Sunday, he was just like them. What had soured his view of the place was that he was married to an Angel Dust junkie.

It was just the kind of social categorizing the English like to think they are so good at that Geoff had come to the USA to get away from. In the Old World everything has a place and every place a name and nowhere are there finer distinctions than in England where the universe has been divided and subdivided and the basis of the subdivision is language, where words either conceal or betray you and escaping from them altogether – escaping your class – is a high art; few ever do it. Geoff had simply bought a plane ticket to a place where he was neither nobody nor somebody. He was whatever he called himself: a boat-rigger, a barman, a ticket-puncher at Kennedy Airport. He found it refreshing to be rid of that minute appraisal of people and behaviour that is second nature to the English, to have no family standards to live up to, no guilt for not being Editor of the *Financial Times*. Everybody in the United States, he found, was in the same business, that of making money, so in a sense they were all equal, however much they made. The country was straight-forward as a Monopoly board. There were no nuances of education, no patronizing jokes and, apparently, no need for polite irony. When you went into a bar it wasn't necessary to ask permission when you ordered a beer, to be careful not to adopt a form of address that cast the barman in the role of servant; you told him what you wanted – 'Give me a beer' – and he gave you one. Geoff had become acculturated. His children went to the local public school; his wife's family lived in the neighbouring blocks. He had exchanged the oppressive scrupulousness of England for the casual venality of New York. It hadn't been difficult. All it had cost him had been his friends.

'I keep the dictionaries and the reference books down in the cellar,' he said. 'With the bugs. Alice doesn't go down there. She says it's dirty. She just raises hell when she finds them in the house.'

'Why not in the closet?' I said.

He grimaced. 'I already have enough crap in there.'

Geoff Morse had not found it as easy as he had thought to shake off that fusty fastidious morality. Exchanging a love of cricket for a love of baseball hadn't been so hard. But the sense of there being a correct and an incorrect way of behaving had stuck. He had tried it Alice's way, which also happened to be the raw Old American way: small-time entrepreneurial capitalism that exploits vulnerable markets for profit, bordering on theft. In Africa they had bought a thousand Seconal caps over the counter at local prices. 'They'll fetch a dollar a piece on the streets of New York,' Alice bragged. I said, 'You're supplying the means for kids to fuck up their lives; you're lining up casualties in the City Hospital.' Geoff said, 'The kids will get goofballs anyway. How people fuck up their lives is their own business. You can't stop them.' He probably never said a truer thing in his life. I said, 'That's shit,' and thought of Harry Lime. It was a couple of years before I saw either of them again. And now they lived on Broadchannel, Queens, in a beautiful wooden house between Rockaway and the Jamaica Bay bird sanctuary. Geoff, now out of uniform, wore a white collar, gave orders in the PanAm terminal, despised Alice's long trips to the 'store', which could mean anything from dropping methadone – legal junk – round at her sister's to shoplifting with her in an invulnerable junkie haze. Now Geoff was on the other end of the dope business. One of the casualties himself.

'I'm here to stay.'

'A closet Englishman!' I sneered.

'Maybe so. If I am, no way can I "come out".'

'What's stopping you?'

'The door's locked. From the outside. Alice has the key.'

'Kick the thing down!'

The gimlets were beginning to work, boring their small lethal holes into common-sense reality. Geoff had found himself in the circle of Hell which – in the language of medieval theology – was exactly in proportion to and commensurate with his error: having turned his back on his own he was doomed to pass his days amid the alien corn, nostalgic for the country which in exile he had come to love.

The bar had been slowly filling up around us with office-workers come in off the street to be alone with themselves and a bottle of imported beer from the fridge before taking on the subway.

'The irony is,' I said, 'you're only sticking it out because you can't see what else you can do – because of that damned sense of obligation and personal responsibility you came here to get away from. You can't leave the kids with Alice – they wouldn't stand a chance. You can't take off with them – she'd follow you and kill you. Anyone else . . .' And here I thought of myself '. . . would just take off, walk out of the whole mess.'

We finished our drinks in silence. Having reached that point in the conversation that we often did lately, we were up against the usual parting of the ways. Between old friends there are issues that have to be returned to, ruminations that go on for years, for as long as they know each other. Marxists would call it their dialectic, the sharp point of the con-tradictions between them. Lovers wouldn't call it anything but go to bed and be damned. For Geoff and me this conversation – usually in some bar – was the axis of our friendship: brief, intimate, pointless.

The barman looked at us and murmured: 'You fellers ready for another?' Geoff hesitated because he had to join the evening shift out at Kennedy; in a couple of hours he would be sitting in front of the video-monitor in the PanAm terminal control-room co-ordinating the arrivals and departures of the jumbo jets. Playing with Dinky Toy aeroplanes on the kitchen table was something he loved doing even when he was a little boy. I hesitated, because the third drink is always the one that gets you there and I had somewhere else to get to. We must have hesitated too long because the barman was already replacing the empty glasses with fresh paper napkins. To me Geoff said: 'One for the road?' And to the barman: 'This man's on his way to Kentucky.'

'He'll have to quit drinking these limey things down there,' the barman said. 'That's bourbon country.'

I looked at him as if this was news to me. 'Yeah? How would you recommend I drink it?'

'Some like it sour, but for taste, straight over ice is how I do,' he said. He turned, leaned deep into his top shelf and pulled out a bottle with a plain white label and some handwriting on it – 'Old Forester' – from which he poured two slugs into the glasses on the paper napkins. 'Try it!' he added threateningly. He rapped the mahogany with his knuckles, jerked his thumb towards himself and walked away from us to serve another customer without touching any of the money that lay on the bar.

Geoff smiled for the first time since we had hit the bar. 'You can't help liking the place,' he said.

We talked about Kentucky for a while – the kind of smalltalk that plays its part in leave-taking. It wasn't so bad for me; I had somewhere to go, people to meet, strangers in strange bars. Geoff had a house in New York, two cars, a wife, three children and a divorce lawyer's bill to pay for.

'I wish I could come with you,' he said. Discreetly he passed me a hand-rolled cigarette from his shirt pocket. 'Take this. In case of emergency.'

I took the grass joint and filed it carefully inside my address book under 'J' and wound the rubber band around it. After that there wasn't any more to be said. We downed our Old Forester. Geoff left a dollar bill on the bar for the barman or the Philippino, whoever got to it first. We gathered my grip and my straw hat and stepped out of the cool air-conditioning of the One Fifth into the sweaty arm-pit of 8th Street and Fifth Avenue.

Christmas Decorations

Somehow I was never able to sleep off the afternoon in the muggy Louisiana heat like the other guests, but that may have just been because, unlike them, I didn't have anyone to sleep it off with. I was alone. Not for me the louvred-shuttered room and bottle of iced wine propped in the crook of a sleepy lover's arm. In the damp shade of the courtyard of the cheapest hotel in New Orleans I sat in a sarong writing letters or else reading the *Times – Picaynne*, sipping cold whisky out of a melamine beaker because there's a State law against drinking in public out of a glass one. For company I had a pair of bees the size of hummingbirds and a small gecko pinned to the wall like an incredibly life-like brooch. After the variega-tion of the gardens where I came from – so suitable for the kind of treachery I was used to – there was something shockingly frank about the flaunted violence of the tropics, the unconcealed daggers of palm fronds, roots coiled in patches of sunlight like basking snakes – or, even, the other way around – the sinister voodoo lily which will probably have the bees for breakfast, and the gaping labia of orchids. It was a place where nothing happened for a long time and then everything did all at once. The leaves sweated and the sweat steamed and rose until the sky couldn't take it any more and then, in the shank of the afternoon, the grey clouds exploded into great gobs of water which fell back down onto the city,

17

flooding the courtyard, running off the leaves, smacking on the corrugated iron roof over my head like the clack of an old tin typewriter, that most irritating of sounds.

One afternoon Pauline got caught in it while she was sweeping the courtyard and was forced to take refuge in my iron arbour. Luckily I had a supply of melamine beakers. 'Hi!' she said, shaking water all over me like a dog. 'I'm Pauline!' I told her I already knew this, and my name, which immediately made us friends. I poured her a shot of Old Crow. She leaned on her broom and chatted to me, drinking it whenever she remembered to.

'What are you always writing out here every day, clickity-click?'

'Letters, things like that,' I said.

'You're not writing a book then?'

I loved the way she got to the point.

'Not that I know of.'

'And you carry that old machine around with you every-where?'

'It keeps my company. I need something to talk to.'

She grinned. 'Well you can talk to *me*! It's too hot to work!'

Pauline worked every afternoon, whatever the guests did. She was a country girl from North Carolina, now the one who cleaned rooms and washed bathtubs after people had sudded them, checked in the new guests and kept the old ones happy. She was young, black and garrulous.

'I write too, y'know,' she told me as if this was something to brag about. 'Though I can't sit down and do it like you do. What do you write about?'

I shrugged. 'Things that happened to me. Things that didn't.'

'I write about my dreams. I get up in the night and just *have* to write them down.'

'What kind of things do you dream about?'

It was her turn to shrug. 'Oh you know, the usual things. Having a family. Owning a hotel in New York City. Going to Australia . . . .'

I stopped the flow. 'Why Australia?'

'I want to write about the Aborigines. They live in big families. In something they call Dreamtime.'

'I hear most of them have been woken up from it. They

18

don't live anywhere any more.'

'You mean they're treated badly?'

I finished rolling myself a cigarette and offered the tin to her. She took the one I had rolled.

'People try to make out it's different here,' she said, exhaling smoke as if she was trying to blow out a candle. 'They say black people aren't discriminated against any more since Luther King's days and the legislation. But's not so different than it was. You just have to look at the Black Neighborhood of New Orleans to see that. And *we* have a black Mayor here.' She added: 'But I guess you spend most of your time over in the old French Quarter . . . .'

I couldn't deny this. Over there there were more bars than you could shake a martini at. I wasn't even sure where exactly the Black Neighborhood was located although the very first piece of advice I had been given when I arrived in the city – from the white taxi driver who had picked me up – was to steer clear of it: 'You wanta knife stuck in you, go down to the Ghetto.' I repeated this to Pauline and she looked at me as if it was me who had said it. 'If you want to see the Black Neighborhood, you come with me. I'll show you.'

'I'd love you to.'

'I come off at five. Meet me here and I'll take you round. It isn't far.' I said she had a date and, waving to her, watched her run back to her work. The rain had stopped while we had been talking. Our acquaintance had taken no time at all to get started, like one of those exotic swamp plants that sprouts up in about as long as it takes you to pronounce its name.

Like everyone else I had succumbed to the charms of the old French Quarter, which are those of the once-famous faded beauty forced to make a living on the streets; hard-nosed realism lies behind the looks and the flair which had once been sufficient on their own. Between its status as a preserved museum town and a real one, respectable and bawdy at the same time, her favours can be had for mere money, which is still cheap, no matter how much it is. In the land of pasteurized milk and honey substitute, New Orleans peddles the Real Thing: the coffee and the beignets in the Café du

19

Monde are fresh-made every morning and the fruit down on the quayside is not the uniformly-sized mush they grow up in California – you can taste it. The bars, it goes without saying, will build you any cocktail you care to name. The elegant two-storey brick buildings with their delicate iron lacework are on a human scale that is comforting to European eyes. In fact, I kept wondering why there were so many US citizens in the streets; it was like Florence in August. A lot of them were middle-aged men wearing the toy uniforms of the US Army Veteran's Association that was holding its Reunion in New Orleans this year, hearing from the President himself which Central American country was a threat to the country's security. Naturally I hadn't run into any Creoles or Cayjuns – what would they be doing in the overpriced bars and oyster parlours? They were out scratching a living among the bayous and on the oil rigs. It was like being in a recently occupied foreign city: cocky teenaged sailors in dixie-cup hats with pretty girls on their arms. I found myself waiting for them to break into a song-and-dance routine: 'There Is Nothing Like a Dame'.

At night the lights come on in Bourbon Street. Everyone is drunk but you hardly notice it – you probably are yourself; when everything possesses the same quality it becomes invisible to the eye. The old Absinthe Bar where Mark Twain drank insists you buy at least two drinks 'per set' – a set being a medley of tired rock numbers played on a Japanese keyboard and drum machine – and the braless bargirl with the neon smile hustles you to get in the second drink before you are halfway through the first. You try another bar; here you have to state your preference for a glass over a melamine beaker but you don't complain; in some bars if you want a glass you have to pay for it. At the door a fem cop with a cigarette between her lips and a gun on her hip sits on a stool checking the ID of suspected under-age drinkers. In the street you join the throng of tourists and sailors and vets milling up and down, deciding where to spend their vacation pay, all of us under the impression we are having a riotous time. At intervals outside the massage parlours a barker shouts the cost of being served a drink by topless women and bottomless men; he swings open the door for us to glimpse the spread legs of naked girls lying on the bartop, one of whom is sucking off a live python.

Pauline guessed right, that *was* the picture visitors took away from New Orleans: the French Quarter, the jazz, the mint julep in the secluded courtyard. Tourists generally inhabit the world of the postcards they send to the folks back home. The more adventurous might stray into the tumble-down residential streets that take over imperceptibly from the bars and the brothels, and wonder why it is that beautiful buildings look so much more enchanting when they are in a state of disrepair and ordinary people live in them than when they are maintained at the expense of the City Council. Or they might sit at the rough and ready tables in Buster Holmes Restaurant, eat gumbo and oysters and drink beer alongside local black house-painters, watch their tentacle fingers swatted by the waitresses, Fats Domino on the ju'box. That, at least, was as adventurous as I had been.

At five o'clock Pauline was in the courtyard. From the shade of the balcony outside my room I watched her waiting. She was wearing a pair of tight blue jeans and a checkered pink shirt with her hair down. She was also wearing lipstick. I realized I had better step into a pair of white shoes, and quick.

We said 'Hi' to each other and started walking. In two blocks we were in the Ghetto, although that wasn't what Pauline called it. In American cities, apparently, the very rich live cheek-by-jowl with the very poor; all you have to do is cross the street to get from one to the other. Usually, though, you don't.

The district we were passing through had once been a white middle-class area. The façades of the two-storey wooden buildings dazzled white in the white heat, carpentered double verandas shading the raised stoop in front, behind which, through open doors, dark shapes moved among the darkness. A white empire abandoned to its black servants. The weatherboarding on many of the buildings had rotted, the paint was peeling and the sun and the rain had leached from the wood all trace of the underlying grain. Several buildings were uninhabited and others had simply fallen down. The gardens, prising open the cardboard-filled windows, were making themselves at home in the front parlours. In the

21

streets, which had not seen a road gang in years, dogs nuzzled trash-cans that overflowed onto the sidewalk and ragamuffin children played in abandoned wheel-less autos and, from the steps of the stoops, grinned at Pauline who called things out that made them laugh. She greeted every person we met and that courtesy was always returned.

We walked randomly, down whichever street took my fancy, but still ended up at the destination Pauline had aimed at, like a card trick in which I had made every decision except the one that mattered; I knew I would never be able to find my way back to the hotel on my own. The door carried no indication of what lay on the other side of it but, inside, Pauline called the barman by name. It sounded like Labàt. He appeared to know her. It was hard to tell. In the Black Neighborhood, as far as I could see, there wasn't such a thing as a stranger. There followed a moment of cross-cultural confusion: we ordered a couple of bottles of imported beer; Pauline started to pay for her drink even though my money was already on the bar. 'Listen! In America you buy your own drinks,' she explained. 'Unless you make it clear you want to do something else.' Just the reverse of the convention *I* had been brought up to observe.

The bar was fan-cooled and deliberately under-lighted. There was scarlet fur along the front of the bar-counter and kumquat orange velveteen-textured paper on the walls. In contrast to the interior, everything inside was brand new and shiny. Paper Christmas decorations hung from the low ceiling. The place was neither full nor empty; a few old-timers played rummy at a table. Pauline was the only woman and I was the only white person but that fact didn't panic the barman who had a nice grin and a nasty squint which he used to some effect; while your attention slid after the wandering eye onto the shelves over his shoulder he fixed you with the lethal gaze of the straight one. The old one-two.

'Well, what did you think of the Black Neighborhood?' Pauline asked me over her drink, her eyes on me.

I said the first thing that came into my head: 'Why doesn't anyone collect the garbage?'

She did have beautiful eyes.

'Do you see piles of garbage in the white areas?'

'But there's a black Mayor.'

'He does his best but he has his work cut out staying in office. The reason is, there are no jobs for black people.'

I said, 'What's that got to do with the garbage? People need their streets cleared whether they have a job or not.'

'Maybe where you come from. Nothing gets done here without you pay for it first with dollar bills. You get the picture?'

I was getting the picture. The roads were in bad shape because there weren't the taxes to pay for them. You buy your own drinks and smoke your own cigarettes.

'Why d'you think there are realtor's notices up everywhere? And the front porches are falling into the sidewalk? Who's got the money to spend on them?'

I didn't know. I didn't care either. 'Don't you have government improvement grants?' I said.

'You mean spend white taxpayers' money on black housing?' She laughed in my face. 'Nothing gets spent on black anything. For years white people said we were animals; they said we *liked* living like this. Now they say things are changing but I didn't see any changes yet.' Her eyes scoured the bar, as if she expected to see evidence of them in Labàt's premises. 'Why d'you think they have Christmas decorations up in the bar here?'

I shook my head. It wasn't a question I stood a chance of getting right.

'Because they're cheap! They don't cost hardly anything. There's no money here. And no work. Look at *me*. I have no money *and I have a job*! The people who own the hotel are real friendly. A white couple who think they aren't prejudiced. They *say* they aren't prejudiced. Hell, I don't give a damn if they are or not, but they drive a Toyota hatchback and *I* don't! I work every day of the week for them, Sundays included, seven to five, and they pay me Government minimum wages. They say it's all they can afford. With a system like that, who needs slavery?'

I asked her what her plans were, seeing as how she wasn't happy at the hotel.

'I'm going to New York,' she said, brightening. 'To open a hotel of my own. I used to live there once. I found a place on 25th Street already and I spoke to a man who might front the money. If he don't, I'll get in touch with the Small Business Bureau. I'll raise the ante somehow.'

23

'If you can't beat 'em, join 'em,' I said but she didn't take offence. Pauline was bright as a button, a single woman from North Carolina who had been to New York and dreamed of going to Australia; she scrubbed floors in a hotel and swilled bathrooms yet entertained the notion of opening her own place in the big city. In this country you can entertain what the hell notion you like. It seemed very natural that she was unsatisfied with her situation; she was also angry about the conditions of black people everywhere and she explained that by the racism of white folks – something in their hearts, not in the heart of American society. She had the anger and the vision but no qualms about making a go of it herself. If she succeeded it would be because she took her breaks, exploited the freedoms open to her in American society. Like everyone else, all she wanted was the same opportunity to make a profit. Pauline didn't have to consider joining them; she was one of them already.

Just then a big fellow in an open white shirt hove to, smiling. It wasn't a good time to ask Pauline who was going to wash the ring from the baths in her hotel on 25th Street. Pauline and the big fellow said hello to each other and he nodded to me. 'Scuse me. Don't I know you from some place?'

'Could be. I get around,' she said.

'Didn't you use to work at Buster's?'

'Well, I did. Yes. I gave it up a few months back. That white guy who bought Buster out started treating the waitresses bad. I told him what he could do with his damn job . . . .'

'Yeah, I heard something like that,' he said, then: 'My name's Grant. Let me buy you both a drink.'

We introduced ourselves. Grant bought some more beer, but no money passed from him to the barman, I noticed.

'Are you looking for a job?' he asked Pauline.

Pauline didn't hesitate. 'I'm *always* looking for a job!'

'Ever you need one, Pauline, you get in touch with me.' Grant handed her a card which she stuck in her back pocket without reading it. He didn't mention the line of work he was in and she didn't ask. Whatever the rules of the game they were playing by, both parties were sticking to them.

Grant invited us to join his friends who were drinking at one of the tables and we did. I was introduced to them by Pauline as someone from England, to make it clear I wasn't a

24

Yankee. Nobody gave me any funny looks but I knew I was only there on her say-so. Grant's friends smiled at us and waved us into some empty seats. They threw me some questions about where I was from and where I was headed but nothing I couldn't field. They weren't in any hurry to give me their life story either. Glasses of Southern Comfort arrived. Away from the bar I didn't know what the form was for ordering drinks; I hadn't seen any signals to the barman and no money surfaced. After a while someone produced a grass joint and eventually I found it in my hand.

The bar, I noticed, was warming up nicely as people drifted in, including one or two women. The juke box was playing old and recent soul and reggae numbers. A current hit came on which had originated in England: '. . . I'm gonna rock down to/Electric Avenue . . .' which struck me as funny. Electric Avenue was where I bought my fruit in Brixton Market when I used to live in Atlantic Road; so-called, people said, because it was the first street in London to have electric lighting, which is unlikely enough to be true. I had to smile, imagining myself trying to explain this to my new friends, that I knew where Electric Avenue *was*! There was no way I could have bridged the grimy reality of the Victorian brick street I knew with the elevated state of mind these cool black dudes were in. But it gave my presence among them a certain legitimacy, as if I wasn't just a tourist.

Grant, meanwhile, was beginning to show a bit of attention to Pauline; he was making her glow. I got the impression he was trying to persuade her to go somewhere with him. Pauline wasn't going to say one way or the other. They were just playing with each other. It was a nicely balanced situation. Here was a man who had a job to offer her; on the other hand, it wouldn't be easy for her to walk out on me under the circumstances. What would she do? I watched for the outcome as if I were a spectator, until I remembered I was one of the participants.

Grant leaned towards me. 'Pauline says you're a writer.'

'Well, I own a typewriter.'

'What kind of things do you write?'

I thought of the rain clacking on the corrugated iron roof over my head while I had sat asking myself the same question.

'Lies,' I said. 'Mostly.'

25

He looked interested.

'I write stories – fiction – things that didn't happen, only as if they did.'

With mock seriousness he said: 'You mean, like the Mayor's speeches?'

Finally Pauline announced it was time to make a move. Grant suggested he drive us home but Pauline batted away his offer. We said goodbye to everyone and they all stood up and told us it was nice meeting us, as if they meant it.

'They're okay guys . . . .' Pauline said when we were outside. 'But you don't want to play games with them.'

The Black Neighborhood didn't look so bad by the light of the moon. There were no street-lamps, of course, which meant you couldn't see how beat-up everything was. Lights from the front rooms silhouetted old folks sitting on the porches, watching us, as if we were walking through the pauses in their conversation. We could smell the dinner they had just eaten.

'You want to see the people who used to live in these houses?' Pauline asked matter-of-factly.

I looked at her, her beautiful eyes, her silver lips, wondering where all this was going to lead. Willing enough to find out, I followed her through dark alleys until, on the other side of an elaborate gate made for a team of horses to pass through, we entered another city. Crystalline in the moonlight, almost luminous, the old cemetery looked like an expensive suburb experiencing a power-cut. Pauline took my hand, leading me through the marble architecture, plaques and family vaults on elaborate biers, elevated to keep them off the swamp. We stood out of our own thin shadows to read the names and ages of the occupants, the dates of their coming and going, which were so precise you couldn't help feeling they were all there, under the marble, the Samuels and the Susannas; waiting for the current to be turned back on. Pauline couldn't resist pointing out how in New Orleans the houses of the Dead were in better shape than those of the Living. She sniffed at the air. 'You smell that?' she whispered, meaning the soft stench of uncollected garbage drifting across from the black streets. 'It's *them*!' She nodded towards the graves. 'Coming out to make our acquaintance!'

Arm-in-arm, we spooked each other back to the hotel, and for the first time in the day I began to feel cool.

After the Fair

It was a pretty warm afternoon and the leather headband of my straw hat had absorbed about as much sweat as it was going to; the stitching had rotted in places and the band was sliding over my ear and beginning to get on my nerves. Overhead the sun was white-hot in a cloudless sky, forcing its way through the fine plait of the panama so that minute shards of light scratched the eyeball. As I roamed the grid of the streets I was forced to step in and out of the light and shade, never in either for long enough to become accustomed to the other. I was getting hot and bothered. It was all a futile dream, one in which I was required to traverse the surreal canicular landscape of deserted boulevards and piazzas of a foreign city on some hopeless meaningless quest. All movement, except my own, took place out of the corner of the eye, deep in the shade, never directly in the field of vision. Is that a dead horse over there? Or just a heap of garbage bags?

Against a wall, well out of the heat, a line of people, some black, some white, stood waiting, purposelessly it seemed to me – but perhaps there was a bus stop somewhere around that I could not see – and motionless like so many stains on the wall, merging into each other. I was lucky to see them. I approached and addressed them as a traveller would the Chorus in an Attic tragedy, as if their only reason for being there was to direct me to the fate awaiting me.

'Can any of you folks recommend a good bar around here?' I said, smiling. I had to repeat it; none of the good people appeared to understand me or know of a bar or, if they did, to care to say. When they got round to answering, their words were vague and from where I was standing out in the sunlight it was hard to tell which of them was speaking. Under my hat, my hot brain had difficulty finding purchase in their intonation, which rose and fell at points in their utterances that were new and strange to me, as if I had learnt my English from books and was trying it out for the first time. My open smile didn't buy me any friends either. I was beginning to feel less like the guileless traveller in straw hat than the leering out-of-town dope-pedlar in sinister sunshades and bad taste white jacket. Finally I was motioned a few blocks off the main street to a building that had an unlit neon sign out front. But the place had run out of business by the time I found it. There was a padlock on the gate with dust on it and a foreclosure notice too faded to read. I must have misunderstood the directions. The good people had no reason to deliberately mislead me.

Knoxville – 'Soot City' they call it and, they also tell you with amiable pedantry, the third largest city in the State of Tennessee – is a hard place to find a beer. Until I located The Diner situated in a pleasantly run-down corner of the city that had not been razed to make way for the 1982 World's Fair, I had walked most of the streets of the old centre, some of them twice. The main thoroughfares are wide enough to carry four lanes of traffic but I jay-walked unharmed across them. Traffic signals directed invisible vehicles. According to Samuel Barber's cantata entitled *Knoxville 1915* there used to be streetcars and horse-drawn buggies. People in pairs, not in a hurry. Autos. Where had they all gone? It wasn't a Sunday. The shops weren't doing any business because, apparently, there was no business to be done; many of them were boarded up, closed down. The dusty windows of the handsome old stores that had once serviced the carriage trade were posted with out-of-date 'Last Sale' bargains. A Chinese restaurant called the Golden Dragon had a sign up saying 'OPEN' but this may have been some kind of subtle Oriental joke, and it was difficult to believe the claim of the Tennessee Cinema that Howard Keel would be starring in a showing of a 1951 musical

30

called *Showboat* 'Tonight' – a sign someone had been paid to put up thirty years ago but not to take down. This might also have been how long it had been since the trains had been running; looking over the concrete bridge that connected the two sides of town, I almost saw a thriving railway junction, tracks criss-crossing, engines and railway stock about to be shunted into place; a passenger train waited at the platform for the green light. It was just a trick of the light: the elegant station was abandoned, the platform deserted; the engines and rolling stock were rusting in their tracks, grass growing between them. The yellow letters 'Southern Railway Serves The South' painted on the side of the carriages were as faded as the truth of that proud boast; you could hardly read them. It looked as if Southern Railway had long ceased paying out dividends to its East Coast shareholders and been foreclosed in the middle of the afternoon schedule. No one had even been interested in acquiring the assets; they had just let it all lay.

The derelict station, like most of the old downtown section, was fixed in a rigor mortis of past usefulness; shapes flitted among the shadows here and there but it couldn't be said the place was inhabited. The impression that people no longer wanted to live in this part of town was reinforced by the new tall buildings to the east: orthogonal Venusian World's Fair constructions, a giant mega-globe and the expensive hotels thrown up to host a transient population. A freeway loop on stilts cut across the city like the dreadful scar from a dangerous necessary operation. Knoxville had recently undergone some major surgery; its vital organs had been replaced by artificial replicas. It had been transformed into a Conference Centre, one of those places that depends for its prosperity on cartel-constructed hotels that guarantee a standard minimum-quality accommodation for businessmen, siphoning off the wealth of other, richer cities. Where local industry had declined the franchise commodity and service companies had moved in: Hilton, McDonalds, Texaco. If you had ever wondered how it was you could cross the United States without ever encountering the family hotel, the home-made hamburger or locally-brewed beer, in Knoxville, Tennessee, you can see the reason with your own eyes: the miracle of capitalism regenerating itself on its own corpse.

I was so badly in need of cooling down I must have been getting delirious because the idea crossed my mind of making it over to the Hilton or the Holiday Inn where they would put something into a glass for me. But Knoxville wasn't so bad I was ready for a muted stringed version of 'The Girl From Ipanema'. I preferred my own nightmare to someone else's.

I circled back in the direction of the railway tracks as if I had business down there: the gunslinger I gave evidence against has been released from prison, he'll be arriving on the next train. I turned a corner and there they all were: people, men and women, moving about, carrying boxes out of stores, loading them into trucks, more activity than I had seen in the rest of the town.

I cut down the shady side of the street. It consisted mostly of second-hand stores reselling farm-workers' clothing and equipment, agricultural gear, 78 r.p.m. records. I ducked into an open door of one of them that turned out to be a shoe-repairer's, cool as a church porch and comfortably cluttered and unswept as shoe-repairers always are. A white-haired old man in an apron addressed me across a huge antique cast-iron stitching machine: 'What can I do fer you son?'

I bid him good afternoon and handed him my hat and let him draw his own conclusions. Without further dialogue he started to hand-stitch the band where it had come loose. Without looking up he said, 'You're from London?' as if he was giving me a piece of information he thought I should have.

'Yes. How did you know?'

'It says here.' He nodded down at the flat panama. 'Hale & Jackson – Hatters to Her Majesty The Queen – Albemarle Street, London W1.'

'I bought it second hand,' I said.

'Nice hat, wherever you got it.' Then: 'You know, I went to London one time. I was there during the War. I was with the 8th Airborne Division, stationed in a place called Suffolk. You know Suffolk?'

'I know it quite well.'

'I spent two weeks in London. Real friendly place and good people. I stayed in Clap Ham. You know Clap Ham?'

'I know a woman who lives there,' I said. 'She's my dentist.'
He handed back the hat. 'What do I owe you?' I asked. I was
learning to talk plain when it came to discussing money. He
waved me off.

'You just say howdy to Clap Ham for me,' he said, 'Next
time you visit your dentist.'

'I certainly will.' Then I got to the point. 'Do you know a
bar around here? I need something to drink.'

'If you want to drink beer, you can't do better than Del's
Diner. Just three doors downaways.'

We grinned at each other. I thanked him and left.

From the outside Del's Diner looked like a drugstore. Only
the row of men drinking beer inside told you it was some kind
of bar. They were seated on a row of cream and lime-coloured
plastic stools fixed to the floor and facing a matching plastic
counter – the original 1950s plastic that was always moulded
to look like marble, as if no one had been able to invent a way
of making it look like itself. The counter faced a dusty image
of another counter in the long mirror behind it, in which there
was another perspex sandwich larder and another soda
fountain. Overhead a couple of large-bladed fans moved the
warm air around the men, all of whom wore denim work-
pants over t-shirts, and baseball hats, though it had been a
while since any of them had played any baseball. They didn't
have to look up from their newspapers when I came through
the door; all they had to do to see me was look straight ahead
into the mirror in front of them. I walked the length of the bar
behind them, taking comfort from the boxes of washing
powder, make-up, candy bars, that were stacked along the
nearside wall. I climbed onto a vacant stool opposite the
Stranger in the white jacket and flat-brimmed hat. He looked
hot and mean and as if he meant business. I knew exactly how
he felt.

There were some out-of-date World's Fair calendars and
beer advertisements over the mirror which I read while I
waited for the barkeep to find the time to make it all the way
down to my end of the bar. Meeting me halfway he looked in
my direction and made an upward jerk with his chin. I ignored
him behind my dark National Health sunglasses. We glared at
each other. Eventually he took a step nearer and – as if I had
made an offer to fistfight him – said, 'Yeah?'

33

'Gimme a beer,' I pitched. I had never spoken to a stranger in such a way in my life, even one wearing a white baseball hat, but it worked.

'Millerfalstafforbud?' he bunted to the outfield.

'Falstaff,' I guessed.

'Large or small?'

'Large.'

This finally got him moving towards first base. He opened the wooden fridge door and took out a beer. I had to pull the tab on it myself but it was cold and wet, you had to say that for it, and it only cost 65 cents whereas a Budweiser will cost you a dollar most places.

I ordered a sandwich and read the side of the beer can while I waited for it:

Now is the Time
    America
Congress is back in
    Session
Millions of people are
unemployed – from
    autoworkers
to construction workers –
and your help is needed.
Write the President,
your Congressman and Senator
and urge them to put
our people back to work
by making it economical
    TO BUY AMERICAN
Please write. Your message
    is important.

I didn't know whether it was a poem, a prayer or an advertisement, though it's been a while since anyone cared about the difference one way or the other. But it was certainly brilliant. Whatever reservations you might have about the theoretical basis of monopolistic capitalism, you have to grant it has horse sense. I had often had to consume the product at the same time I did the advertisement, but this was the first occasion I had had to drink from a can of beer carrying an ad

34

for a system of political philosophy. I found myself wondering what Falstaff would have thought of it.

The sandwich arrived and I put it in my mouth. The barkeep placed a fresh can on the counter and swiped away the empty one.

'Give the young feller a glass, Del!' the man in a baseball hat on the stool next to me told him, although none of the other drinkers had a glass and I didn't particularly want special treatment. I didn't have any choice. Del put an iced pilsner glass next to the can and walked away from it. I almost thanked him but I managed to stop myself in time.

Behind me, at tables arranged around the far corner, a group of black folk were sitting but I didn't get the impression it was because they wouldn't get served at the bar. I could have been wrong. A woman who had children waiting for her somewhere sat alone at a table holding the handles of her full shopping bags, as if she didn't want to give the impression she would be staying. On the other side of the table an old feller – blind and drunk – was murmuring a slow blues, clunking his beer can on the table top every bar. 'Them good times . . .' Clunk. 'Are gonna come . . .' Clunk. 'One of these days . . .' Clunk. He was a prophet crying in the wilderness. No one paid any attention to him.

'What brings you to Knoxville, son?' Baseball Hat said, turning his head to look at me, or rather at my hat.

I didn't feel like telling him I was brought by a piece of music, and one that wasn't Blue Grass or Rock 'n' Roll: *Knoxville 1915*. For me Sam Barber's elegy summoned the flavour of this town on a particular summer's evening before the sinking of the *Lusitania*, the traffic of ordinary citizens going about their business, parents in porches, a tranquil toing and froing of neighbours and animals, street-cars . . . . '*A horse, drawing a buggy, breaking his hollow iron music on the asphalt; a loud auto, a quiet auto; people in pairs, not in a hurry, scuffling, switching their weight of aestival body, talking casually, the taste hovering over them of vanilla, strawberry, pasteboard, and starched milk, the image upon them of lovers and horsemen . . . .*' It was a tableau I knew by heart. And though I didn't feel like admitting this to the old-timer on the stool next to me, it wasn't improbable that his ma and pa had been there that evening, part of the tableau.

35

'I'm just passing through,' I said evasively. 'Heading for a place called Pigeon Forge.'

'You going up there to see the Smoky Mountains?'

'I wasn't planning to, no.'

'You should see them. They're purty. You be seeing the Elvis Museum?'

'Not that either.'

'Can't say as I blame you. Well, there's the Smoky Mountain Car Museum. Contains the actual Kill Car of Big Sheriff Pusser. They made a song 'bout him a few years back. "Walk Tall . . . ."'

'I remember it. But I don't expect I'll see any of those places. I'm just staying over. On my way down South.'

'Down South?' He mulled that one over. Then: 'What you think of Knoxville?'

'It's a big town,' I said guardedly. 'Hardly any people in it though, as far as I can see.'

The man cackled. 'Plenty of people, don't you worry. Folks call us suspicious but we ain't so bad when you get to know us some.'

He smiled at me and I couldn't help smiling at him. He wasn't your two-hundred-pound Southern redneck, more out of the Wiry Prospector mould, a face pitted and creviced as if something had been prospecting in it. I wouldn't say he had a warm smile but he had some kind of one.

'If you would have been here last year I coulda showed you some people. The World's Fair was held right here in Knoxville. I never did see so many folks in all my life as was here then.'

'How did it go, the Fair? People have a good time?'

'Some say so, some say no. I didn't get to see much of it m'self. Couldn't afford to. But I heared a heap of folks was disappointed. They came a long ways to see it, from every State in the Union to do their vacationing here in Knoxville.'

'That's hard to believe on a day like this. The place is deserted.'

'Oh they all stayed in the new hotels. There was a whole village built for them. Some people in Knoxville made a lot of money outta them folks. All they cared about was money. Prices went up to the sky . . . .' He looked up as if we could see them up there. I said something like you have to expect that sort of thing. He looked at me angrily. 'You know how much they were charging for a parking spot during the Fair? Six dollars.'

I shrugged. 'Is that a lot?'

'*For one hour*? It may not be where you come from but it's plenty for Tennessee, let me tell you. It made me sick, son, to watch my own town skin those folks. To tell you the truth I was ashamed for Knoxville and I was borned here.'

I didn't know what to say to that. I had tripped a fuse. I said something and waited but it appeared to be the end of the conversation. We joined the rest of the hatted drinkers in reverie, a row of different-coloured baseball hats and a straw one By Appointment To Her Majesty bent over beer cans, as if we were at a pew, praying for something. In back of us the blind man clunked his can on the table. The Good Times are gonna come. He didn't bother to tell us again and no one said Amen. The life had ebbed out of the place. I found myself shivering. My sweat had cooled sufficiently to feel as if it belonged to someone else.

Suddenly I wanted to be outside, in that warm sun. I finished my Falstaff and left a quarter on the bar, saying goodbye to my neighbour as I slid off the stool. He didn't reply, but I think that was because he hadn't heard me.

It felt cooler outside, cooler than it had been before, that is. It had become that time of evening when people sit on their porches, rocking gently and talking gently and watching the street and the trees, parents on porches, uncles and aunts, and from damp strings of morning glories the dry and exalted noise of locusts . . . .

But there were no porches and hardly any people in the street. I took a stroll along the railway tracks from the crossing towards the station, to investigate the scene I had previously looked at from the bridge, walking between the carcasses of the freight trains. I climbed aboard a caboose and looked at the sad scene until a voice from someone I couldn't see hollered what was I looking for. I hollered back 'Nothing' but it wasn't really true; that was what I had found.

The music that had brought me here didn't celebrate any other world except this one – streetcars, autos, asphalt – assuring me that things in their places did not need any justification for being there; they certainly didn't need the painstaking seeking after the validity of their existence that so wearies you where I came from. What I had found in Knoxville, in the lee of the World's Fair and on the back of a beer can, wasn't any different. And I was a foolish tourist to expect anything else.

Back in the Greyhound bus station I sat dully waiting for my bus, trying not to listen to the voice thanking me for Going Greyhound that sounds so sincere until you realize it's a taped recording being played in every Greyhound station in the country. On an impulse I made a telephone call and while I did someone filched my hat. I couldn't help smiling. This was more like it, the America I felt at home in.

Whoops!

The sun flashed on the white front of the old Palace Hotel on Market Street, fading the already faded painted pueblo-style frieze decorating it. Some of the windows were half-open. On others green baize shades were lowered. In the cool rooms behind them guests would be sleeping off the hot heat or just lying on their beds sipping cold beer under the fan. The hotel – at four storeys one of the most palatial buildings in Silver City – looked just right: elegant, run-down, cheap. I stepped out of the heat of the highway into the shade of the sidewalk and put down the lighter of the two pieces of luggage I was carrying in order to push open one of the double plate-glass doors with a free hand, wedge it with my foot, pick up the piece of luggage and release the door behind me – nimbly, before it shut on me. I'd like a room please. Sure. For one? That'll be nine dollars fifty plus tax. In advance. Fine.

But for some reason I couldn't get the door open. It seemed to be stuck. To get a better pull on it I set down the second, heavier piece of luggage. Nothing. It wouldn't budge. Through the glass I could plainly see a foyer, the registration desk, a grand sweeping staircase, a packed valise, two red leather upholstered barber's chairs, one of which had an unread folded newspaper lying on it. I could see there was something funny about the scene but what it was – the absence of any people, staff or guests – did not immediately suggest to me any obvious conclusions. My hot head was already lowering itself onto the pillow of one of the beds in one of the cool rooms. Nine dollars fifty plus tax. In advance. Sure. Just as soon as I get this damn door open. I gave it another firm tug.

'Hey!' a voice piped just behind me. 'The place is closed up.'

I turned around. A gangling tow-haired boy was silhouetted against the street. He was hugging a brown paper grocery sack with both arms.

'You looking for a room or something? You won't get one here. The Palace closed up a couple of months back. It's a real shame. Did you just get into Silver?'

While I was fending off the boy's questions I saw – or rather, from the voice, heard – that he was in fact a girl, a young woman in running shorts and running shoes. But skinny, not someone you would have thought could run.

'You look wonderfully crumpled,' she said. 'Where are you from?'

I told her where I was from and picked up my two pieces of luggage. She began to saunter off along the sidewalk, listening, as if she assumed I was going the same way she was. At the corner of Market and Main she stopped. I stopped. She said, 'Well. . . .' I said, 'Well, maybe you could point me at a bar. Some place I can sit down.'

'Right here,' she said, indicating left. 'Here. Let me.' Shifting the groceries under one arm, she took the lighter of my two pieces of luggage out of my hand. 'DAKOTA ATHLETICS' was printed across the front of her tank top. I followed her past a store selling firearms and through an open door that had a hand-painted bison over it and the words 'BUFFALO BAR'. We parked ourselves on a couple of empty stools. There were about fifty to choose from. The place was the size of a small cinema. Over the mirror over the bar was the stuffed head of a bull buffalo.

The young woman behind the bar came up and placed coasters in front of both of us. 'Hi Jo! How ya doing?' she said.

'Hi Gail. I'm fine I guess. I didn't see you around for a while.'

'I been away visiting. I only just came back from Kansas City a couple of days ago. By the way, I saw Travis while I was up there.'

'Travis? I thought he was in St Louis. How was he?' Jo asked.

42

'Oh you know. *Juggling!*' They both laughed. Gail smiled in my direction: 'Hi! What can I get you?'

'Whatever beer you have on tap,' I said. 'And . . . ?'

'I reckon I'll have a glass of milk.'

'Sure.' Gail served us our drinks on the paper napkins and left us to it.

'As you can see, everyone in Silver knows everyone. Especially Travis.'

'What does he juggle?'

'Juggle?' She pulled a face. 'Oh. Money. Time . . . .' She rolled her eyes towards Gail and back again. 'And, of course, *Girls!*' Then: 'By the way, my name's Jo-Anne.'

I took her hand and introduced myself. We were both pleased to meet each other.

'So what brings you to Silver City? Most nobody ever makes it up here,' she said, a thin white moustache of milk on her top lip. She licked it off.

'The name appealed to me,' I said. 'Silver City has a nice ring to it.'

'Is that the only reason?'

'It isn't a reason.'

'You're an intuitive type, huh? Well you have pretty good intuitions. Silver's a fine place. Still the good old mining town it always was. Small, funky, and it has a real wonderful climate. What sign are you?'

'Scorpio,' I said.

'That explains it! What about your rising sign?'

'Scorpio as well. So they tell me.'

'Jee-zuz! I better watch out! Me, I'm just a lousy Cancerian. Anyone can push me around.'

I glanced up at the stuffed buffalo head on the wall. I could have sworn one of the eyes winked at me.

'Are you from Silver?' I asked Jo-Anne.

'Me? No. I'm from Des Moines, Iowa. I'm over at Western New Mexico University . . . .' She waved an arm in the direction of the rest rooms. 'I'm doing my Master's there. Say, why don't we take your bags over to my place. I'll show you round. We'll fix you up some place to sleep, don't worry.'

'Look, I don't want to put you to any trouble . . . .'

She shut me up with a bat of her wrist. 'It's no trouble. And

43

let's face it,' she grinned. 'Against a double Scorpio I don't stand a chance! You wait here. I'll get the truck.'

Abandoning her groceries, Jo-Anne ran out of the bar. In her Nike running gear. I ordered another beer from Gail and read the sign across the bar which said 'Definitely No Fighting'. Next to it was an old Coca-Cola ad, one of those painted 1950s saucy poses: a girl falling off her roller-skates, showing what she was wearing under her skirt. 'Whoops! Silly Me!' The damn bull buffalo winked at me again. This time I winked back.

Silver City was a small friendly-looking town – of 10,807 inhabitants, so the population post on city limits specified. Two- or three-storey brick commercial buildings,some of them mosaic-inlaid and with wooden verandas, fronted graceful brick-and-adobe residences. Flowering trees hung over garden walls. Beyond the walls washing soaked up the sunshine. Beyond the trees the brown Mogollon Mountain range looked very near in the clear air. I leaned an elbow out of the open window of Jo-Anne's old Ford Ranchero as she drove us east through Silver City, giving me a pocket history of the place over the music coming out of the tape-deck. There was a 'No nukes is good nukes' sticker on the windshield. The shelf over the dash was a mess of Winston cigarette packs, old parking violation tickets, unfolded maps. Also a paperback copy of Prescott's *History of the Conquest of Mexico*. I resisted the temptation to fold the maps or pick up the book. We turned into Bullard Street. Bruce Springsteen was dishing it out: '*Can't start a fi-ya. Without a spark. This gun's fer hi-ya. Dancin' in the dark* . . . .'

'A lot of these banks and stores were built with mining money,' Jo-Anne said. 'Some Forty-Niners heading back east found silver here. In those days this was all Apache country. Cochise and Victorio, those guys. Fact the man who founded Silver – John Bullard – was killed by Apaches. Rough justice, huh?'

It seemed pretty rough to me.

We stopped by the City Museum – a small mansarded Victorian mansion – in order that I could inspect the pre-

Collumbian ceramic relics of the Nimbres Indian culture in which Jo-Anne had some particular interest. There were many other exhibits in the museum. One which particularly interested me was an old wind-up painted tin cowboy on a horse with a mechanical lassoo.

'Visitors come to Silver because it's where Billy the Kid grew up,' Jo-Anne said when we were back in the truck. 'They come to visit his mother's grave. They're more interested in that little murderer than in a culture that was here a thousand years before him.'

'What are you doing your Master's in, Local History?'

She laughed. 'Well I guess I am in a way. My subject is archaeology. I'm doing my research on the Nimbres Indians. We're excavating a Nimbres habitation up in the Gila Hills. Trying to figure why they vanished. I'm working on dating techniques.' She glanced across at me and grinned. 'And not the kind you learn in High School!'

'I never learned any,' I said. 'But then I never went to High School.'

We stopped outside one of the houses in Sixth Street. Inside, the house was a mess. 'Sorry 'bout the mess,' Jo-Anne said but not as if she was especially. We walked through the front room to the kitchen. There were piles of unwashed dishes in the sink. Jo-Anne had run out of washing liquid. She lifted two cans of Coors from the fridge, handed me one, and we carried on through to the backyard where plastic flamingoes stalked round a blue plastic toddler's paddling pool. They looked jokingly convincing in the long scrub grass. The ancient Mustang belonged to Travis who was away over in Kansas City. Or St Louis. There was a black astronomer's globe on the front seat, lolling like the head of a passenger with a broken neck. We were sitting under a green-barked tree which Jo-Anne called a Palo Verde and she said the big fluorescent green beetle buzzing us like a tiny World War One fighter's plane was a Palo Verde Beetle. The other tree, with eucalyptus-like leaves, was a China Berry tree, she said. Jo-Anne knew the names of the flora. At college she had followed a Plants & Society course. Also Spanish, Astronomy, Economics, American History. To me the different subjects she had studied seemed as unconnected with each other as the bits of junk in her backyard but to Jo-Anne they

45

all led to what she was doing now: Archaeology. Who said it was junk anyway?

The telephone rang inside the house. Jo-Anne said, 'Excuse me' and went inside to answer it. She was away quite a while. I waited, watching the red ants crawl in and out of my shadow.

She came back and we sat talked some more. Then she said: 'Why don't you take a shower and rest up while I fix something to eat? If you like we could drive up to the mountains and watch the sun set. We could visit my friends Steve and Louise's place and take a dip in their hot springs. How does that sound?'

She had a soft voice that made her sound younger than she looked. She looked about eighteen.

'Sounds great to me,' was all I could think of saying. Somehow it didn't seem enough.

'Travis says if you half-close your eyes Silver looks like Florence from here,' Jo-Anne said over the steering wheel of the Ranchero.

Route 90, signposted for a place called San Lorenzo, climbed away from town towards the hills and the Nimbres River. I looked up from the map, half-closing my eyes as Travis suggested, and looked down over Silver City, red-roofed with the late sun behind it and green among the red-earthed green hills. There are a lot of places in the USA that look less Tuscan.

It was cooler now. Jo-Anne was wearing Penny Ranchwear jeans and a faded Fruit of the Loom sweat-shirt. I wasn't feeling so wonderfully crumpled.

The road started to climb. We drove until the wild oaks had to struggle to get a foot-hold on the side of the hill and then there was only cactus and scrub and rock. Then there was only rock. Jo-Anne said: 'Y'know, these hills are becoming a desert. The Anglo cattlemen overgrazed them. All they thought about was sending the beef north before they lost the contract. I don't blame those cowboys, but now the grass has gone, the top-soil is eroding. In spring the water runs down those little valleys – *arroyos*, the Spanish call them – creating

46

flash floods. Fact, one of them swept away near every house in Silver's Main Street one time.'

Plants & Society. Spanish, Economics. American History.

'Rough justice,' I said.

Jo-Anne pulled over. We got out and climbed, first down then up, picking our way among the scrub and rock. 'Watch out for snakes!' she said over her shoulder. She looked like a boy again. Skinny.Moving sure-footed among the rocks. I lumbered clumsily behind her. 'Hey, watch out for jumping cactus!' I was panting when we reached the summit but she wasn't. We sat down and smoked cigarettes, watching the sun set, a flaming apocalypse in the distance that had nothing to do with us. Someone else's farm was burning. It was like being in a Marlboro advertisement, except we were smoking Winston.

'I like it here,' Jo-Anne said softly. 'When you leave the highway you step back before the Apaches. The Nimbres Indians lived up here for centuries. Then they vanished. In about the twelfth century, we reckon. We don't know why. Maybe a real bad drought. But the whole of Mogollon culture disappeared off the face of the earth.'

Unless, of course, you counted the round ceramic bowls in the City Museum that remain unbroken, that you could still store things in if you cared to, as useful and fragile as the day they were made.

The breeze tussled the scrub grass and Jo-Anne's stubby yellow hair.

'I sometimes feel,' she said, 'that the USA is just balanced on this earth like a house of cards. Wendy's, Shoney's, McDonald's, the banks, the shopping malls, the automarts. They're all just made out of plastic and pasteboard, without foundation. A real big wind could blow it all away. Pouff! No different than what happened to the Nimbres Indians.'

'No nukes is good nukes,' I said.

'Right. If we make a hero out of Billy the Kid, we gonna end up like him.'

We drove down to Steve and Louise's spread on the Nimbres River Commune. Steve and Louise weren't at home but we walked through their place anyway until, at the edge of their vegetable patch, we came to a wooden hut where we took off our clothes in the near-darkness and slid into the hot

47

opaque water of the little concrete pool. There was hardly any moon. We could just about see each other's white face under the light of the zillion stars. Jo-Anne, astronomer, identified some of the constellations: '. . . the Big Dipper . . . the Little Dipper . . . Cassiopeia's Chair.' From the black bushes came the frantic ratcheting of crickets. We soaked for a while, shooting the breeze, our toes now and then touching under the water. She wanted to know whether I believed the stars had any influence over the destiny of human beings. I told her I had an open mind which she thought was a typical Scorpio answer. That, I pointed out, only proved they did. When our fingers began to pucker we got out and dressed and drove back to Silver. It was about ten o'clock.

The Buffalo Bar was full of cowboys when we got there. The boys from the Lazy-Z were in town. We had to edge around them to get at the bar but I didn't get the impression that this was because they were deliberately trying to stand in our way. They just didn't seem to see us. It looked as if their minds were on something else.

We took our glasses of Coors to one of the empty booths where it was quieter, or at least not so noisy. On the other side of the wall, in the dance hall next to the bar-room, a band was murdering some old Eagles numbers. Jo-Anne explained that the hall used to be a hardware store until it went bust and The Buffalo bought it up, punched a hole in the wall and turned it into a place for musicians to play. Over in our section the juke box was belting out Country & Western songs. I couldn't see why they didn't brick up the walls and have two separate bars.

Because there were two separate clienteles. Besides the cowboys and a few women drifting around, there were a number of wide-shouldered fellers wearing black or white muscle shirts that showed off their tattoos. They were nearly all wearing plastic baseball caps, the kind the gas stations give away free, and clipped Burt Reynolds moustaches. They looked a lot meaner than the cowboys.

'So this is your local bar,' I said to Jo-Anne.

'Yeah. Well, Travis likes it. It's not usually so lively. It can get pretty rough.'

'Why do you come in here then?'

'They know me here. I get carded in most bars I go into. They think I'm under-age,' she said. 'And I'm a Cancerian. I guess I'm reckless.'

The cowboys were standing facing the bar or on stools leaning back on their elbows against it, the slope-heels of their tooled Spanish horse-riding boots hooked onto the foot-rail as if that was what they had been designed to do. Some of them were young and some of them not-so-young but they made up a posse. They shared pretty much the same idea of what a man wears when he goes into town on a Saturday night: tapered plaid shirts with studded pockets, ironed, tucked into leather belts and denim pants. Judging from the prevailing fragrance, they also shared the same can of aftershave. You couldn't help noticing how recently razored they were. But they weren't your Nashville cowboys. The pick-ups parked at an angle outside were specked with mud and cow slurry, and you couldn't see any gallon stetson hats or fancy chrome-studded vests. They were all together and also isolated, as if still separated by the open spaces of the chapparal. They sat quietly drinking beer and smoking cigarettes. One or two were playing pool, circling warily around the table as if it were some kind of mean-acting steer.

'Cowboys come in here weekends once in a while,' Jo-Anne said. 'They work over in Sierra County so they usually head for Truth Or Consequences to spend their pay. It's a funny kind of life they live. In trailers mostly.'

'Why are they so morose?'

Over the bar-mirror the red eyes in the stuffed bull-buffalo head were flashing on and off. The buffalo was getting lit up on whisky fumes.

'Morose. That's the word for them. Marriage is my guess. Women are a pushover for cowboys but it never seems to work out. A trailer's no kind of a home. I guess that's why they're a dying breed.'

'Like the Nimbres Indians.'

It was time to return to the bar to get a fresh pair of beers. Holding both glasses in one hand, I sidled through the crush, taking care to give a wide berth to the wide-shouldered pool-player in the red Texaco baseball cap lining up the white ball with the pink in the far pocket. The girl he was playing against was dressed for the beach: halter-top, short skirt, rubber thong sandals. She looked as if she was in a different game to him completely. One in which she was the prize.

I couldn't get at the bar for cowboys. Gail was serving way down the other end of it. While I waited I looked over the shoulder of Texaco-Cap sighting his cue ball. I might learn something. He brought the cue back and as he did a hand gently pressed into the small of my back – I could feel the separate fingers – and nudged me forward. I couldn't stop myself from pitching on top of the pool-player. I had to put a hand against him to steady myself and, as I did, one of the glasses I was holding in the other hand slipped out and smashed on the floor. Before it did I heard the cue strike the cue-ball. I was already turning round to put a face to the hand when the butt-end of the cue-stick rammed backwards, smacking painfully into my hip.

Looking back, I saw a couple of cowboys leaning against the bar, gazing into the middle distance. Over their shoulders I caught sight of the Fifties print of the girl on roller-skates showing her panties. Whoops! Silly me! Definitely No Fighting. The pool-player turned me around by the shoulder as if it were a closet door he was opening.

'What's your problem, dickhead? Ain't the bar wide enough for you or what?'

'I'm sorry,' I said. 'I guess I lost my balance.'

'Go lose it some other place!'

He pushed me backwards with no more force than had pitched me into him in the first place. As I recoiled, I jammed my elbow into the belly of the cowboy behind me. The cowboy caught me and righted me. Then he said: 'This feller you're pushing around is a friend of mine.'

It began to dawn on me that I had been set up. I was a thirteen-amp fuse between unearthed kilowatts, a blue Hawaiian sportshirt with white sailboats across it caught between a black muscle shirt and a plaid one with studded button pockets.

'Well can you try keeping your dickhead friends from falling over the pool table!'

'My friend is no dickhead, I don't believe.' The cowboy glanced towards me for confirmation of this but not as if he cared one way or the other. I was speechless.

50

The cowboy gestured me aside with a polite wave of his hand. My role in History was over. It must happen to Belgium all the time. The two men stood looking into each other's eyes.

An arm circled my waist and gave me a yank – it was Jo-Anne. She propelled us deliberately between the cowboy and Texaco cap. 'Excuse me,' she said. With automatic politeness they stepped back for the lady and Jo-Anne marched me away from them. I waited for the crunch and grunt of punches being thrown but it didn't come.

'I can see I'm going to have to watch you, Scorpio!' Jo-Anne said.

Gail appeared at our booth with a pitcher of beer. 'Some feller at the bar sent this over.' She shrugged. 'Said he owed you it.'

We couldn't drink more than half the pitcher. That stuff turns your brains to cotton balls. The band was still thrashing itself to death in the dance hall and one or two of the redneck girls and their fellers were even dancing to it but the cowboys were drifting off. Back to their trailers on the Lazy-Z. And we did too.

Outside, Jo-Anne backed her Ranchero away from the other old Fords. There were parking meters all along the street which had been decapitated and turned into flower baskets. A cowboy was legging up a girl in a halter-top and short skirt into the cab of a Chevvy Cherokee next to us. She was wearing white panties. Whoops! Silly me! Definitely no sign of Texaco-Cap.

Silver City. Rough justice.

Jo-Anne drove us back to Sixth Street. We were feeling pretty high. We had a smoke and she thanked me for a great evening. Then she made me comfortable in her bed and rolled a sleeping bag out for herself in the back yard between the Palo Verde and the China Berry tree. I lowered my head onto the pillow and dreamed that Jo-Anne was in a hole in the ground, in an excavation – she was handing out to me a perfectly preserved Nimbres Indian ceramic bowl, which I was about to hand over to the Cowboy – and that just then a telephone had started to ring. Taking the bowl out of my hands, the Cowboy passed me the telephone receiver and I said hello into it. It was the operator. She wanted to know

51

whether I would be willing to pay for a collect call from St Louis, Missouri. I said, Sure and a voice said:

Hi! This is Travis.

Hi Travis.

Who is this?

It's a long story.

I guess it is. Is Jo-Anne there?

Sure. Right now she's asleep. Outside in the yard.

Outside? Well when she wakes up tell her I'm okay. I'm on my way home.

Sure.

Thanks pal.

So long.

So long.

Pointers and Setters

The front lobby of the Hotel Grim was vast and magnificent. White corinthian columns supported the ironwork balcony of the mezzanine and chandeliers were suspended on chains from the moulded ceiling on which there was some delicately ribbed plasterwork. It was all done in the Classical style, elegant on a scale that lifted the heart, a perfect place in which to listen to a Chopin piano recital. Shades were lowered over cathedral-sized windows and the light filtering through them was softened and made cool by an expanse of white marble floor. The lobby was empty except for three black old-timers sitting in armchairs in front of a silent television picture, each of them reading a newspaper. The sound of water from the recent downpour rushing along gutters outside almost drowned out the rustle of newspaper pages being turned.

Behind the registration desk the room clerk was sitting at an ancient telephone switchboard – the kind into which the calls have to be plugged by hand – sweating in her too-tight jeans. She looked flustered. Her sleeveless voile blouse was sticking to her skin so that you could see the style of brassiere she was wearing underneath it. Somehow she didn't give the impression that she knew what she was doing – a change from a lot of hotel personnel you have to deal with – but this may have been because her girlfriend, on the near side of the desk, was flustering her.

'8–4–7 . . . 6–4–9 . . . Quick! Before he comes!' the girl-friend was urging her.

'Lois!' she said over her shoulder. 'I just dialed it! There's no tone even!' She was young. Too young to stand up to Lois, anyway.

'You have to dial three-zero-two *first*!' Lois told her.

The room clerk picked up a ballpoint to write the out-of-town code on a pad.

'Don't write it down, dummy! D'you want *him* to see it?'

Lois – she wore a lemon-yellow halter-top and turquoise terry shorts – was leaning right over the top of the desk so that her legs were off the floor. One of her moulded plastic sandals was hanging on to her foot from the arch of her toes.

The room clerk dialed the numbers again. She didn't ask who 'he' was. After a moment she said: 'There's still no reply!'

'Well God-damn! I don't believe it!' Lois said. She put on a face to express Indignation. She was acting the part of a woman in a TV series, *Dynasty* or *Dallas*, who didn't ought to be treated this way.

The room clerk approached the desk and I asked for a room. She began to turn the pages of her ledger. She looked up at me and said, 'You want a room for two?'

'Why would I want that?' I said.

'Aren't you two together?'

'Who two?'

I looked at Lois. Lois motioned over my shoulder with her eyebrows. Behind me a tall skinny white man in dark sun shades was halfway across the lobby. He was carrying two small pieces of luggage, one of which looked as if it was a violin case.

'No. Just for me,' I said.

Lois said, 'It ain't often we have to handle such a rush!'

I waited while the room clerk filled out the space in her ledger. She wore a gold medallion in the shape of her name – IRENE – on a gold chain around her neck. She said, 'That'll be $9.50.' A stricken look crossed her face when I showed her my MasterCard. 'I'm sorry. We don't accept credit cards. We . . . don't have any facility . . . ' She made a see-for-yourself gesture with her hands towards her side of the desk in case I didn't believe her. 'Don't you have cash?'

'Sure,' I said. 'I have a ten-dollar bill. I had to give away my spare to a gas station attendant. He didn't accept credit cards either. Is there some law in Arkansas against them or what?'

'This isn't Arkansas,' Lois reminded me. 'It's Texas. But I like your shirt.'

I was wearing a colourful Hawaiian sportshirt.

'There's a bank right opposite,' Irene said helpfully. 'Only it just closed. Ten minutes ago.'

It was twelve after five. I took out my last bill and offered it to Irene. 'There'll be some place in town I can buy a fifty-cent hamburger,' I said.

'Don't bank on it,' Lois said. 'Not in this town!'

Irene didn't know what to do. It was one of those situations people were always putting her in.

Then the violin-carrier spoke. 'I reckon I can front the man a ten. If that's what's holding things up,' he said. He was standing behind me next to one of the corinthian columns, beside which he had placed his luggage. 'I'm not going to be leaving before ten.'

He peeled a twenty out of a clip and handed it over to Irene. 'You can take for mine out of that,' he told her. Irene gave him her lopsided smile and I thanked him as well as I could. She gave him a dollar back and he handed fifty cents of it over to me. 'Your change,' he said.

Irene said: 'I'll put you both on sixth floor. No-one will bother you up there. You can have an entire corridor each!'

She went over to the key-board. Lois, who was leaning back against the desk with her arms outstretched along the length of it so that the outline of her yellow halter-top was nicely profiled, started in on the violin-carrier. 'Hi! How long you planning to stay?'

'Just until I get my ten dollars back,' he said.

'Did you come in a car?'

'Is there any other way?'

'Sure. There's a Trailways. Only that doesn't get in till a quarter after eight. Say, did anyone ever tell you you look like Mick Jagger?'

'Everywhere I go,' he said, deadpan. 'I'm saving for a skin-graft.'

Lois giggled. 'So where're you headed? Nashville?'

57

'Nameless, Tennessee . . . . Some place where they never heard of Mick Jagger.'

'Oh, I didn't mean to. . . . No offense, you understand?' Then Lois nodded towards the violin-case. 'Are you in the music business?'

'Nar. I just use that to carry my machine-gun around in.'

Irene was holding the keys, happy now that it was all settled. She had one of those odd-shaped mouths that look sad whether its owner is sad or not. It had just always been that way, from way back, and made you feel sad yourself, looking at her. As if she had a hair lip.

We took the keys to room 611 and 625.

'See you around,' Lois called after us.

There was a bad smell in the elevator, of old sweat and must. We introduced ourselves to each other. 'I'm Karsten,' he said. 'It's a German name. My parents are German.' There was a handwritten notice pinned to the elevator wall: 'All visitors must not use this elevator after eleven pm without they report to the front desk. Order of the Management.' At the sixth floor we went opposite ways down the connecting passage between the H of our separate corridors. 'Come by for a smoke,' Karsten said over his shoulder. 'If you feel like one. Later.'

This is how I come to be sitting in Texas, naked under the fan in room 611 in the Hotel Grim, showered, smoking a cigarette, looking out over Arkansas. The room is high-ceilinged and spacious and most of the space is filled with torn and patched pieces of furniture that no thrift shop would ever accept – the rotating armchair I'm sitting on for example. The fan, which isn't one of the latest designs, is humming and wobbling because the dial has been set on 'max'. I'm shivering and sweating, both. One of the panes in the window is made out of plexiglass and another is cracked and the rest are wedged with strips of scotch tape. Through the window – because the room is on the sixth floor – I am able to look down onto the yellow overhead traffic signals at the deserted intersection between the flat roof of a brand new white-walled Exxon gas station and a brand new white-walled First Federal

Bank. Beyond city limits a flat expanse of hot shale and sagebrush grass and desert shrub stretches as far as the horizon, over which an almost transparent moon is rising into the blue.

Down below, here in Texas, the boulevard is still glistening after the downpour three-quarters of an hour ago. It's steaming. Over in Arkansas a man with a brown paper sack under his arm is walking out of a store that has a pink-and-lilac neon 'Liquor' sign in front. I watch him cross the boulevard and pass under the electronic clock outside the First Federal Bank on which the time – 5.49 – is alternating with the temperature – 84°F. The man crossing the state line is wearing denims and a black t-shirt. He's carrying a six-pack across the border from a State where it's legal to buy one into a State where it isn't. In the puddles on the roof of the bank small birds are bathing, fluttering their feathers.

At the intersection an old open-topped white Montego slows to a halt in front of the man, although the traffic signals are on green. A woman in a lemon yellow halter-top hangs out of the car and the man stops to talk to her. He must have one foot in Arkansas and the other in Texas.

The figures of the clock flick from 5.49 through 5.52. The man and the woman speak for exactly three minutes, after which the Montego glides off. The man continues on, disappearing below my line of vision. I sit watching the deserted boulevard, the small birds bathing, the moon rising over a flat landscape of banks and gas stations – the light turning to copper – until there's a knock at my door.

I put a towel round me and opened the door. A man in a black t-shirt stood holding a brown paper sack.

'Hello. Come in,' I told him.

'Well . . .' Karsten hesitated. 'You're dressing. I figured you could use one of these.' He pulled a bottle of imported German beer from the sack. 'Come by later. When you're ready.'

I told him I sure would.

Later, when I came by, Karsten was lying shirtless on top of one of the twin double beds, propped up behind a copy of

Rolling Stone, his bare feet crossed, sticking out of the end of his jeans. He was still wearing his sun shades. It was the kind of picture of a picture of a rock star that you see on the front cover of the magazine he was reading. 'Hi there! Good to see you,' he said. He waved me in with the *Rolling Stone* which he folded and tossed onto the chair between the two beds. 'How's your room?'

'Pretty much the same as this one. Shabby. Ornate. A bit smelly. I quite like it,' I said.

'Push that over here and make yourself at home.'

'That' was his open violin-case in which a good-looking violin was half-propped, not all the way in, the bow resting on top of it. I lifted the case, still open, off the bed.

'This looks like a fine old fiddle,' I said.

Karsten swung his legs over the side of his bed and took the case out of my hands. 'It is. Real old. Nineteenth-century Italian.' He lifted the violin out of the case and laid it on the bed. 'It was my mother's father's.' He tapped the thing as if it were a pet dog. 'I never let it out of my sight. I've even slept with it in bed with me.'

He opened the little built-in felt box inside the case where the resin and spare strings are usually kept and took out a single-skin spliff. He lifted it up for me to see and grinned. He had an attractive sexy grin. You couldn't deny there was a certain similarity between his big satyriac kisser and Mr Jagger's.

He lit the spliff with a Zippo and passed it over.

'What kind of music do you play on it?' I asked him. 'Mariachi or Mozart?'

He looked at me. 'As a matter of fact I play both kinds of music. The difference between rock 'n' roll and what people like to call "Classical" music is something that exists in their heads. The border-line is artificial. Like most borders. They're people who don't understand music – a lot of musicians, in fact.' Then: 'What about you? Where d'you stand?'

'Me? I don't stand anywhere,' I said. 'Mariachi *and* Mozart.'

'Yeah?'

Karsten picked up his grandfather's fiddle and played a couple of bars from a scampering fast-time Mexican waltz. Then he stood up off the bed and, with the fiddle still under his chin, moved to the centre of the room where he began to play

60

the slow movement from a Mozart Sonata. He played it as Ry Cooder might have played it. When I realized he intended to play the piece right through I lay back against the pillow and shut my eyes. The room began to smell of fresh-cut roses.

At the end of the piece I didn't say anything. I couldn't speak. Karsten laid the violin and bow back in its case and closed the lid.

'I was able to play that piece when I was eight years old. That was how old I was when I came here. My parents crossed over from East Berlin to West Berlin when it was still possible to do that. Before they built the wall. None of us spoke a word of English when we came to America – not one damned word between us! But I guess it wasn't so bad for me as it was for my brother and my parents. I was just a kid.'

'Where did you end up?' I said.

'We moved around – Wisconsin, Illinois, Ohio. I feel American but not *from* any part of it particularly.' He grinned. 'You gotta keep movin!'

Karsten opened another bottle of Becks beer and handed it across the aisle between the two beds without a word.

'And Mariachi . . . ?' I said, taking the bottle, tipping the neck in acknowledgement. 'How does that fit in?'

'I can play near anything that *can* be played on a fiddle. Bluegrass. Country. Cayjun. But I *like* that TexMex border music. I guess because it comes out of two completely different places. One thing it don't come out of is the fear Mexicans and Texans feel towards each other. I've been an immigrant. I know what it's about.'

We drank beer and talked about things until the light began to thicken and it was time to talk about what we were going to do next. Neither of us felt like getting up and going over to the door to turn on the chandelier.

'That sassy girl. The one at the front desk,' Karsten said.

'Lois.'

'Yeah. That's her name. She hijacked me. She's convinced herself I look like Mick Jagger. What can you do?'

'Don't ask me. No one ever took me for a rock star. Not even for Bill Wyman.'

'I just look foreign. Some girls are looking for Mick Jagger's mug in every man they run into. I get it everywhere I go. They're not always the girls you want to . . . well, you know, *know*.'

Karsten and I left the hotel together, he for his appointment with a girl in a yellow halter-top who drove a battered white Montego, me for mine with a heated-up crawfish pie in Miss Kate's Louisianna Seafood Restaurant. The three black old-timers were still sitting in front of the TV rustling newspapers when we passed through the lobby. Or perhaps it was some other three old-timers. As we passed they wished us a good evening and we were given the once-over by the person behind the registration desk. He was an old white man in a white shirt with old-fangled sleeve-bands – perhaps the 'him' Karsten's date had referred to while she was making her out-of-town telephone call earlier in the afternoon.

Before we parted Karsten asked me if I thought I might not need another ten spot, just in case. I told him thanks, but ten dollars' worth of fun was about all I could allow myself anyway.

My crawfish pie cost a dollar eighty – peas extra. It tasted similar to one I had in Denver. I didn't like having to stiff the waitress but now wasn't the time to start giving money away so I just thanked her.

Outside the restaurant I wondered what to do. There was a busy traffic of roaches along the sidewalk though hardly any on Stateline Boulevard between Texas and Arkansas. The gauge on the front of the First Federal Bank recorded a temperature of 74°. The sun had set and the moon was high. There was a kind of funny smell coming up through the sewers after the rain. I watched the Trailways bus drive along Stateline in front of the moonlit bank.

There was not much to do in Texas so I crossed the border. I soon found that there was only one thing to be done in Arkansas because, unless you got in your car and drove out of town to the motel-hotel strip, there was only one bar – the Arrow Bar behind the Trailways Bus Station.

The water in the air that the customers inside the bar had exhaled dripped onto the new customers' heads as they came through the door because the air-conditioning outlet-fan was positioned exactly over it. This explained the pool of wet on the now dry sidewalk.

The Arrow was doing good business. I had to walk almost the whole circumference of seated pairs of pants at the bar to find an empty stool. But in bars you don't always have a choice where to sit, you have to muscle in where you can. If you're on your own you sit up at the counter – even if you're on your own with someone else. If you're with someone – you're married or lovers or doing business with each other – you sit at one of the tables arranged around the walls. My stool was at the end of the bar near two doors, one of which had 'Pointers' inscribed on it, and the other 'Setters'. It took me a moment to work out what they meant.

I sat down, ordered a drink and lit a cigarette, thinking that it was just this that I liked about bars, joining the confederacy of loners at the communal bar-counter, staking out my own bit of it with my pack of cigarettes and my glass of beer and my pile of money. This lonesome moment.

But it didn't feel as lonesome as the men and women looked who were standing in front of the electronic machines giving out martian muzak, the lonely starship pilot-cadets finding out if they had it in them, the skill to repel an invasion from Mars. I wondered how they could handle so much responsibility.

There were two women tending bar. It was nearly time to order another beer before I realized I knew one of them already. We seemed to recognize each other at exactly the same moment. She gave me her funny lopsided smile.

'Hi! How ya doing? Can I get you another?' she asked me. She looked pretty with her hair up.

'Thanks. I'll have a Bud – from the tap. So you have *two* jobs,' I said.

Irene shook her hair. 'Not really. I just cover for Lois at the Hotel. We cover for each other all the time. Sometimes it *feels* like I have two jobs!'

She disappeared down the bar. There was a sudden crush to get one in. Irene and the other woman bartender gave them all they had but there was still a bit of a panic. Then, almost immediately, the bar emptied. Customers at the bar and at the tables made for the door in ones and twos – singles and couples, leaving the jukebox and war-game machines zapping

63

and crooning after them – until the bar was no more than a quarter-full.

'What happened?' I asked Irene. 'Do they know something I don't?'

'What . . . ? Oh. They're all from the Trailways bus. The New York bus has a half-hour rest stop here. It leaves for Little Rock 'bout now. They mostly all came in on it. Some of them haven't seen a drink since New Mexico.'

'You can't help feeling sorry for them,' I said. Next to what they were about to endure, Room 611 in the Hotel Grim acquired a certain funky glamour.

'Why sorry? They're going to New York, aren't they?' she said over the sink. 'Day after tomorrow they'll be walking out on 42nd Street!'

'You've been there,' I said. Or it may have been a question. In fact the New York Port Authority Bus Station is located right on 42nd Street, the sexiest, meanest street in mid-town Manhattan.

Irene dried her hands on a towel and then began to polish the glasses she had just washed.

'Been there? I *lived* there! – and not just Queens or Brooklyn!' She made it sound as if it was a thing to be proud of. 'I was born on Upper West Side – 96th Street, as a matter of fact. I still have a girlfriend from junior high who writes me now and then.'

'What brought you here? Texarcana is a long way from Upper West Side.'

'My mother moved West six years ago. I was fourteen when she and my father split up. At the time Arkansas seemed like a good idea to the man she was with. He's my stepfather now. To me it seemed like the end of the world.'

'It's nice and quiet here,' I said.

'Quiet? Oh, it's real quiet if it's quiet you're looking for. The half-hour rest stop of the Trailways bus is the liveliest show in town. I hate it. I just hate it.'

'What's stopping you from stepping onto the next Trailways to 42nd St?'

'My husband doesn't like New York. He has a good job working for the Federal Utilities Inspection Agency. Wayne says New York is no place to bring up kids. I tell him, Well look at me! He just laughs and says, You see what I mean!'

We both laughed. Though I'm not sure why.

Irene took away my glass and filled it up from the tap without a word – or any money – passing between us. She kept the bar with more aplomb than she did a hotel registration desk.

'So what's the big attraction about New York?' I asked her.

'It's alive. Things are always going on. Music. Shows. Dance. I used to roller-skate in the Park. From our apartment on 96th we could overlook the Hudson River. I used to climb the fire escape to the roof and watch the *Queen Elizabeth* come into port – just when the sun was coming up. I never saw anything like that in Arkansas. It makes you want to cry, doesn't it?'

'It does,' I said.

'I could go to college I guess, learn something useful only Wayne is dead set against that. He says why invest in education that isn't going to make a return? He says in two, three years he'll make a full Inspector and I can give up tending bar and we can have kids. He doesn't understand. Say, I hope you don't mind me telling you all this?'

Irene fingered her gold nameplate medallion on its chain around her neck. She looked so lost and pretty it did make you want to cry. She was too young to have a broken heart. Her case was worse, hers had never been whole in the first place. It made you want to carry her off through the night in a two-seat Camaro all the way to the ocean.

'I don't mind. I'm just passing through,' I told her. 'This time tomorrow I'll be in Brownsville. You can tell me anything you like.'

'Yeah. You're right. When you live in a small town like this, strangers are the only people you can talk with. I just wish. . . .'

Irene drifted over to a customer along the bar who needed serving. I took the opportunity to pay a visit to the 'Pointers'. When I got back Karsten was sitting on the stool next to mine.

'I found you,' he said, without turning his head.

'Thanks for looking.'

He shrugged. 'You can find things you didn't look for,' he said. He turned towards me. 'Don't you know that?'

65

'What happened to your date?' I asked him.

I caught Irene's eye and signaled with my finger towards my own glass and an invisible one in front of Karsten. Irene gave the counter-salute that she had gotten the message.

'She took me for a ride,' he said. 'Lois has a nice car.'

'Yeah? Where did you ride to?'

'Out of town some ways. Into the desert.' He nodded over his shoulder as if it were right close by where he rode.

'How was it?'

'The desert? It was nice. There's nothing much out there.'

'So everything was nice?'

'Yeah. It was. Real nice. She wanted *me* to be nice too.'

I just looked at him.

'People keep taking me for someone else. Who is this Mick Jagger guy? Is *he* nice?'

There was an edge to his voice.

Irene, arriving with the beers, said: 'I thought you said you two weren't together!' We all smiled at each other. She took some of my money off the bar.

Karsten reached for my pack of Marlboro and lit the cigarette he took out. He held it delicately, his fingers crooked at angles, as if they were about to play a tricky chord on a piano. I found myself wondering which one it might be.

'Lois said she thought you was a fairy,' he said.

'Sorry?'

'You know . . . *gay*! It was your shirt gave her the clue. She said it was too damn pretty for a man to wear.'

I looked down at my shirt but it was no longer the colourful Hawaiian I had arrived wearing.

'That was nice of her,' I said.

Karsten shrugged. 'I told her you *were* one!'

'I see. Well, that was nice of *you*!'

'Hell, I told her I was one myself! She wanted to know if I played fiddle like the guy who plays fiddle for the Velvet Underground. What else could I do?'

I was starting to wonder what form his proposition would take when he said: 'So you like Mariachi *and* Mozart?'

I nodded, unsure just how loaded the question was.

'You're like me. We play *both* kinds of music.'

'Hold on! I'm a non-musician!' I said, choosing to take the man literally. 'I don't play *any* kind.'

'Non-musician? Musician? I don't understand what you're saying. All barriers are artificial.'

'I was thinking the same thing before you came,' I said. 'I was asking myself what Irene would say if I told her there was a two-seat Camaro waiting over the border – room for one to the ocean.'

'Which border you talking about?' he asked softly.

'The one between what you can and what you can't get away with, I guess.'

'Oh that one,' he said. 'I already crossed it. Long ago.' He gave me his sexy Mick Jagger grin. 'So? You didn't ask her?'

'I got to take that right-hand road. There *is* no Camaro. She's happily married to Wayne. I'm going to Brownsville.'

'You'll take the same damned road you always did! Like most people do.'

We finished up with a brace of Wild Turkeys on the house, after which we were ready to croon '*Irene goodnight. Irene goodnight. Goodnight Irene. Goodnight Irene. I'll get you in my dreams . . .*' And, laughing, we left her there looking pretty and flustered – the two things she was good at looking. Then we said goodbye to Arkansas and walked back under the moon into Texas over Stateline Boulevard. '*Sometimes I live in the country. Sometimes I live in the town. And sometimes I have the great notion. To jump in the river and drown . . .*'

The old white man in sleeve-bands looked up at us as we came through the lobby, singing, but he didn't say anything. He couldn't say we were disturbing the other guests – we still hadn't seen any. The TV was blank and the armchairs in front of it empty. In the bad-smelling elevator I thanked Karsten again for bailing me out. He said to forget it. We arranged to meet around ten thirty in order that I could buy him breakfast and repay his loan. We said goodnight and went towards our separate corridors.

> *. . . Irene goodnight, Irene goodnight.*
> *Goodnight Irene. Goodnight Irene.*
> *I'll get you in my dreams . . . .*

Of course, I never saw him again.

On Parnassus

Following the printed sign which said 'POETS THIS WAY', I went out through the open glass doors in back of the lobby to the pool. It was still quite early so the pool was deserted and the pool-side bar was all closed up. There wasn't a poet to be seen. A member of the hotel staff, however, was rearranging the white plastic bucket chairs neatly around the white tables, straightening umbrellas that needed straightening.

'Hi!' she called to me from the shady side of the pool. Her white shirt was reflected upside-down on the surface of the water which was absolutely clear. Alongside it, on the flattened perspective of the blue tiling, a single leaf floated, motionless.

I said: 'Hi! Can I have breakfast out here?'

'Sure . . . why not?' she said. Then, smiling: 'I'll be with you momentarily.' She was a brown white girl with the hotel regulation white shirt and short black cotton rah-rah skirt. She had, too, the short regulation blonde hair and the long regulation brown legs. Like a lot of Californian girls who wait on tables she couldn't help but make you think that this wasn't the kind of life she was ultimately destined for. She was just doing it for now, for pocket money. She was destined to be driven down to Bodega Bay in an open Porsche Carrera. At least.

'I have to sweep here first,' she explained.

'Take your time,' I told her. 'I have this to read.' I slapped a copy of the *Calistoga Gazette* onto one of the tables and sat down in one of the bucket chairs. The floating leaf, I noticed, was in fact a large leaf-coloured moth. It had probably drowned during the night in the reflection of the moon in the water.

The newspaper was full of the schedule of events for the 12th Annual Calistoga Poetry Conference. The celebrated San Francisco poet John Hogan would be giving a reading. There was going to be a seminar on something called 'The Challenge of Language Poetry'. This went some way towards explaining the printed signs all over the hotel and why, last night in the bar, everyone kept asking everyone, 'Are you a poet?' 'Not me, pal,' you'd say or, if you happened to be one, 'Sure. Are *you*?' Then you would get introduced: 'This is Jeff . . .' or whatever your name was, '. . . he's a poet,' or 'And this is Gloria who isn't a poet.' 'Hey, I damn well am!' 'Oh, I'm sorry. I didn't know.' That was how it went on all night. It was a hotel stuck full of drunk poets, some of whom, if the place had been raided, would have been lucky not to have had their poetic licences taken away from them on the spot.

'Okay now. What can I get you?'

The waitress was standing across the table, her pad and pencil at the ready. She was very pretty, with the clear skin and good teeth of a young Californian.

'Just coffee,' I told her. 'Can you bring two cups. My friend will be down presently.'

'Sure. Is that all? Okay.' Then she said: 'I guess you're a poet.'

'Hell, no! I work for a living. Are *you*?'

'*Me*? A poet?' She giggled. 'What a crazy idea!'

'You mean you just inspire the stuff,' I said.

'What?'

'Shall I compare thee to a summer's day?'

'Sure . . . why not?'

'Thou art more lovely and more temperate . . .'

'Hey! Take it easy!' She backed off. Laughing. She returned with two hexagonal white china cups on a silver tray, filled one of them with coffee and then poured cow's milk out of a hexagonal white china jug. That was the kind of hotel it was. When I thanked her she said: 'Oh, you're welcome!'

I glanced through the pages of the *Gazette* until a movement over by the glass doors caught my eye. As I looked up a well-built black man wearing egg-blue swimsuit and trimmed moustache was mounting the diving board. He was massive, a serious iron-pumper. His biceps, triceps, quadruceps, pectoral and trapezius muscles were bunched and bursting. He dove. The flat water split under him and then he went under it. A blonde white woman in a white bikini stepped through the glass doors and took his place on the little board. She raised her hands, lowered her head and slid into the pool after him. The pair of them looked like perfect specimens from two related but entirely different species.

Karen looked fine when she joined me at the table – she was wearing her fluffy punky-pink mohair sweater and white tennis shorts – but I could tell that she was thinking about her husband.

'I *do* like Calistoga!' she said, beaming, to me. It was a habit of hers to make declarations out of the blue that sounded like contradictions of something which had just been said, but which hadn't.

The waitress, arriving with coffee, said: 'Hi! How are you?'

'Hi! Can I have some water?' Karen asked her.

'Sure. What kind do you want?'

'What kind do you have?'

The waitress produced the hotel's fancy gold-edged menu. 'We have Calistoga regular . . . Calistoga with orange . . . with lemon . . . deionized . . . Perrier . . . .'

'I'll take deionized,' Karen told her.

The two perfect bodies glided silently below us through the water, rocking the moth on the choppy surface. Karen hooked out two big pills from her travelling bottle of megamultivites and pushed one of them across the table towards me. 'Negatively ionized water,' she declared, downing the other pill with the water which the waitress at that moment put in front of her. 'Neutralizes the positive ions that build up in the body's thermal-regulation system.' Her declaration hung like a cartoon bubble over the blue swimming pool, hushed except for the little splashes caused by the underwater swimmers.

Karen understood the body's chemistry. Her own showed hardly any wear and tear. Her skin was as clear as the waitress's, without a single worry-line. What had she ever had to worry about? A grown-up child herself, she was about as burdened with responsibilities as her own grown-up children, untouched by the world outside northern California.

'Well . . . ?' she said.

I said nothing, feigning not to know what she was welling about.

'It's not such a big deal as you're making out,' she said.

'It's not the *size* of the deal that worries me,' I said. 'It's its nature.'

'You mean you think I shouldn't go in?'

'You want my blessing?'

'I want you to tell me if you think it's going to be a good idea. Or not.'

'In terms of what?'

'Whatever terms you think important, I guess.'

'In terms of risk accountancy – if you get caught – a month in jail for every grand you stand to make sounds about right to me. Depends how pure the stuff is.'

Karen smiled. 'It'll be the purest!' She made the word sound as if it meant something on the lines of Wholesome. Fine. Apple Pie.

'But in terms of morality. . . You'll have to ask your priest. Ask *him* how pure it is.'

'You know I don't go to church any more!'

'Well, perhaps you should. Could be you're out of practice deciding risky matters like this on your own.'

'There isn't so much risk involved,' Karen informed me. Then: 'Well, no more than you'd expect in a high-yield investment. When you put your money into a new business – if it takes off – you get a percentage of the take. If it doesn't, well. . . . You understand what I mean?'

'No. Do you mean you won't even *see* the stuff?'

'Sure I won't! Stefan says I won't know anything about it. I won't know the other members of the company and they won't know me.'

Stefan was Karen's husband, a Sonoma County dentist and the reason we were in Calistoga, Sonoma County. Or, as she sometimes put it, her ex-husband.

'Then what would your commitment amount to, exactly?'

'$5,000.'

'Is that all?'

'I told you it wasn't a big deal. Did you think I was going to be the one who carried it across the border in my pants?'

'At least transporting the stuff in your suitcase through customs exposes you. To the Law. You have to sweat for your money.'

'I won't be exposed!' Karen said, smiling. It was the smile of a person who had never been exposed to anything more lethal than a foggy afternoon in Pacific Heights. 'But I'll get a steady income from it. No sweat. No questions asked.'

'Or answered.'

'What?'

I gave up. It was a conversation without nuances, comic, flat, being carried on in cartoon bubbles against a perfect blue sky, a blue swimming pool, beautiful swimmers, white tables and green umbrellas, a menu with five different kinds of water on it. It wasn't a landscape in which qualms could flourish. Poetry – maybe.

Karen's ex-husband Stefan had a house outside a small town called Glendale on the shore of Clear Lake, although his surgery was in Santa Rosa itself, an hour's drive away. Calistoga was about the same distance on the other side of the Napa valley. It was a beautiful drive, sunny, verdant, with isolated wooden homesteads and clinics tucked into the side of the wooded hills. The square inch of the Rand McNally Routefinder in which it was located appeared to contain as many State Parks and Recreational Areas as the whole of Texas. Karen, peering through her driving glasses, drove fast on the stretches of flat and slowly round the tortuous bends of the two-lane road. The sunlight strobing between the leaves of the tall Jack pines flecked her clear skin with little shadows like unpleasant thoughts troubling a child for the first time. The Audi compact she was driving had been a let's-call-it-quits present from Stefan – not part of the settlement – but after two years she had still not gotten used to the stick-shift. It was the first car she had driven which had one. Perhaps it was Stefan's little joke: from now she has to handle everything herself. Karen was troubled by the old-fashioned foreign manual mechanism – when all her life an automatic

had done fine – and the fashionable environmental accept-
ability of foreign compact cars. It was a contradiction which her
Arica Therapy Group was helping her to work through. Since
her divorce, Karen was learning to take responsibility for
herself, more and more.

Stefan was a member of the Dental Practitioners' Association of California. He serviced the perfect smiles of the lovely
people of Sonoma and Napa Counties, and the lovely people's
lovely children. I had never met him. I was on edge. Dentists
make me nervous.

I found myself twitching the radio dial in search of a local
music station – we were too far from San Francisco to pick up
the one Karen had it set on. The radio didn't look like a radio
but like one of the technical data gauges of the dash which was
made out of that charcoal-grey high-performance matt plastic
that German car manufacturers specialize in. 'Hey!' Karen
said as soon as the radio had tuned into a station relaying one of
the songs from *Astral Weeks*, 'Leave that on.' She wanted to
catch up on her Van Morrison.

We were driving through a little place called Sonoma
Springs behind a pack of racing cyclists wearing different
coloured skidlids and identical lilac maillots with 'Schwinn
Cycles' printed on the back. They were riding fast in a tight
clump, elbows in, knees pumping. Karen slowed up behind
them while we drove through the town. Sonoma Springs was
pretty. There were no billboards anywhere to be seen and all
the stores and public buildings, even the banks, were wooden,
natural varnished. As soon as we crossed out of city limits
Karen accelerated to overtake the cyclists on an open stretch.
A blue pick-up with some kind of horse-truck in tow was
approaching in the opposite lane. Having committed herself,
Karen was forced to put her foot down to clear the cyclists. It
was a close thing, I thought, but Karen seemed not to notice.
She was what she called an Intuitive-Sensation type.

'I better slow down. Or we'll arrive there too early,' she
remarked.

I was going to make a joke about being in no hurry to arrive
there dead but I decided against it because I didn't want her to
think I was nervous. I turned Van Morrison off.

'You're sure your husband isn't going to mind? Me coming
along?' I said.

76

'Sure I'm sure. Stefan's a very relaxed person. He said it was fine. And stop calling him my husband!'

I called Stefan her *husband* to remind myself that she still allowed him to make important decisions for her. He had paid in full the settlement which the Court had awarded Karen – her return on the seventeen years she had put in raising his family – but a lot of her money was still tied up in his portfolio of investments. Because she didn't know what a portfolio even looked like she was always having to come out to Clear Lake to sign some bit of paper. The only thing Karen understood about money was how to spend it. Where it came from was still as big a mystery to her as where children did before she found out for herself.

Karen had emerged triumphantly from the cocoon of the good American daughter of the two-star Army General, suburban Catholic wife of the successful dentist. Ever since she was a teenager she had been in a state of suspended animation: down to the store, phone mother, collect the kids, down to the store, phone mother, collect the kids. Somehow she had discovered San Francisco. Grass. Sex. And the Human Potential Movement. From these she was learning to put herself in what she called 'syntony' with the Universe. Self-Actualization, the Arica School called it. I called it Having Fun Without Guilt. That's the way it is with these intuitive-sensation types.

'There it is!' Karen said. The road followed her finger round the curve of a promontory into the lake. 'My home for ten years!'

Across the blue water a white villa filled a gap in the green wooded precipice. The outline of the lakeshore cliff merged against the high elevation of the Sacramento Wilderness behind it and, beyond that, the snowy mountains of the Mendocino Forest. It was a vista that must have taken an awful lot of orthodontal bridgework to pay for.

'How do you get down to the lake?' I asked Karen. It sounded like the kind of thing you asked.

'We had some stairs cut into the side of the rock. Stefan keeps a speedboat to run into Glendale.'

A wooden sign said 'HIGH TOWERS' and a printer's hand pointed down a steep dirt track which we took, driving through some luxuriant foliage which didn't look native to

California – if anything still is. When we reached the drive there were several cars already in it – a nacreous Mercedes, an ice-blue Jetta – and children's shrieking voices coming from the direction of a pool. The man in shorts and an open Hawaiian who was playing a hose over the children waved to us. We got out and he laid down the hose onto the grass and came over. He gripped my hand and greeted me by name and said, 'It's a real pleasure to meet you' with a smile that looked sincere. He was well-built and well-tanned. His thinning hair was cropped short and there were some distinguished-looking flecks of silver among the hairs on his chest. Karen said Hi and smiled but didn't touch him.

'Come round and meet some nice people,' Stefan said, ushering me lightly by the elbow. We followed Karen into the garden. Four people wearing sunglasses turned to look at us and wave at Karen. Two men – both dressed in white tennis outfits, white leather pumps, white socks – were standing by a sundial mounted on the balustrade, holding bottles of beer. A woman in jogging shorts and bikini-top sat at a poolside table on which a magazine lay open, and in the pool a younger woman was teaching a small child how to cavort like the others. It was about midday. The sun was almost directly overhead. There was a shadowless perfection about everyone.

Stefan introduced me: '. . . Liz . . . Paula . . .'

'Hello . . . nice to meet. . . . Where you coming from . . . oh really? . . .'

'. . . Tony . . . Fredrick . . .'

Tony Magari, the slightly older of the two men, was Stefan's lawyer, and Paula was his wife. The children belonged to Stefan's new partner, Fredrick, and Liz – in the pool – his wife.

'Think you could use a beer?' Stefan said to me. 'I have ale in the fridge if you'd prefer.'

'Beer's fine,' I told him.

Karen accepted a Calistoga.

I sauntered over to look at the view and give myself something to do. We were pretty high up. Everything there was to be seen you had to look down on. Clear Lake was blue. A pair of windsurfers yawed at parallel angles to the wind.

'It's a big jump,' Fredrick said.

Stefan arrived from the villa with a tray of St Pauli beers. 'What is?' he asked, handing me one.

I stole a glance at Karen but she was over by the pool in conversation with Paula about something in the magazine. So I was alone with her ex-husband and his associates. With the men drinking beer out of bottles.

'The jump from up here to down there,' Fredrick said.

'How big?' I asked. It sounded like the kind of thing you asked.

Fredrick looked at Stefan.

'Oooh, I don't know,' Stefan said. He rubbed his chin as if it was going to be a tricky calculation. 'You'll have to ask my lawyer.'

We all laughed, especially Stefan's lawyer.

'It's a goddamn of a long way,' Tony Magari said.

'Is it the same distance, the jump from up here to down there,' I asked. 'As the jump from down there to up here?'

They thought about it.

'It depends,' Tony Magari said. 'On how bright you are.'

I pulled a face. 'So so,' I said.

They laughed.

It takes a few billion years for the ammonite to evolve into a human being,' Magari said. 'It takes only a moment for some dumb kid from LA to throw himself into the Grand Canyon. It's the same distance!'

'Unless you're smart,' Fredrick said.

'*Unless you've got a good lawyer!*' Magari sneered in a comic, shyster way.

After a while of this a young Philippino in Bermuda shorts appeared at the glass doors. He stood flashing a big struck-lucky smile at us to make it known that it was time to eat. In an air-conditioned conservatory overlooking the lake we ate braised fennel and veal saltimbocca. We ate white and red grape sorbet. We drank champagne from the Buena Vista vineyards at Guernguille.

'You're lucky, Stefan,' Liz said. 'Marco is such a damn good cook!'

'Good cook slash butler slash gardener!' Stefan said.

'You're a real Californian, Marco!' Tony Magari called to the Philppino servant. 'Every Californian has to have at least one slash-occupation!'

79

Marco grinned gratefully.

Later, wearing one of Stefan's pairs of Speedo swimsuits, I dozed on a floating polypropylene raft in the pool while the three men and Karen were jaw-boning in the conservatory and Liz and Paula chatted and sunbathed under the umbrellas. The raft rocked – I felt limp, like a big wet moth – on the waves which the children playing down in the shallow end were setting up. I was trying to calculate how much more St Pauli Girl I would need to drink before the bottle would float in the water on its own, thereby maintaining its temperature, when a small hand grabbed the bottle and a little girl's head popped out of the water. 'Hi!' the girl said. 'Can I taste some of your beer?'

'Sure. Do you want to get drunk?' I asked her.

She thought about it. 'Oh, I don't think so,' she said gravely. She was a nice kid, about eleven years old – what they call a pre-teenager – fair-skinned with freckles, innocent, although the precise line between innocence and knowledge – or even corruption – was becoming blurred. The beer and champagne I had consumed might have had something to do with that.

The sun shone directly into our eyes nearly all the way back to Calistoga, too low for the pull-down-windshield shades to be effective.

'I feel real good. You know that?' Karen announced. She looked across towards me. 'How 'bout you?'

'Me tired. Me fuzzy.'

She grinned, put her hand into the pocket of her pink mohair. 'Here!' She held out a neatly-folded rectangular paper packet, the kind you only have to look at to know its contents. 'Stefan asked me to give you this. He didn't feel okay about giving it to you himself.'

I took the packet and unfolded it carefully over the Rand McNally Routefinder.

'Ooo, goody! Denture-Fix Powder!'

Karen took her eyes off the road to look the stuff over.

'So the deal went ahead?' I asked her.

'Deal?'

80

'The shares deal in the Border Business . . .'

'Oh no! I told them they could count me out. I didn't want to have anything to do with that. I didn't get a good feeling from it. I got an intuition it wasn't such a good idea. That's why I feel so good! I'm learning to stand up to peer-pressure, you know that? You know what I'm saying?'

'I know what you're saying,' I assured her. I took a pinch of the Denture-Fix into each nostril and then rubbed my fingers into my gums. The tall lights of the truck ahead came on and glowed.

The Hotel bar was quiet so I didn't notice at first how quickly it was filling up. I was in conversation with a recent acquaintance at the counter – an old-timer drinking Wild Turkey with ice – and the carpet had muffled the sound of approaching Nike sport shoes. 'It was a dangerously dull life . . .' he was telling me. 'You had to watch out. Some of those people were *ruthless*!' He had just been let out after a ten-year stretch in some institution in Wyoming – not a penitentiary, he said when I pressed him, but some Faculty of Letters which had taken him on as Writer in Residence. He was a nice-mannered, silver-haired old boy, frail and tough. 'Henry Kissinger once said he learnt all he knew about tactics on the Harvard campus. Where the fights are all the more vicious because the stakes are so small!'

One of the seminars or workshops must just have come to an end. Behind us delegates and guests were conferring with each other in different dialects of the same language, polite, sober. One or two of them were even trying to attract the barman's attention. It was hard to tell how well anyone knew anyone, they all looked so different. Most were dressed with bits and pieces put together with inspired taste: silk and denim, political t-shirt and printed crêpe dress, Brooks Brothers shirt and Hell's Angel's leather – different versions of Swap Meet Chic – as if they had rifled each other's wardrobes.

Aside from the poets it was the kind of bar that was always quiet. Classy. No juke box. Paper napkins dulled the clunk of glasses against the counter – a slab of black marble with anodized aluminium rail and insets. The décor was sculpted out of pieces of black glass and mirrors to produce a Busby Berkeley effect. Unless it was from here that Busby got the idea.

'How d'your reading go, John?' a big voice said behind us. A hand laid itself gently on the old-timer's shoulder.

'Oh, hello Tom!' the old-timer – John – said, looking round. 'It went very *well*!' sounding a little surprised himself that it had. Gracefully, he accepted a Wild Turkey with ice from Tom, covering the hand on his shoulder with his own. He introduced me.

'Howdy,' Tom said without offering me his hand to shake. He had Pluto's beard and Popeye's biceps. The smile looked to be his own. 'You a poet here for the Conference?' he enquired.

'Not me. Are you?'

He shrugged. It was something outside his control.

'Near everyone here is,' he said, casting an eye around the bar. 'The New York School . . . the Language Poets . . . the Women, of course . . . . Even one or two Confessionals. It's very tribal.'

We watched the poets slip by each other and congregate according to their allegiances, like pieces of iron filings aligning themselves to the pull of a magnetic field.

Karen appeared at the entrance of the bar, freshened up and changed into her Canal Street black rhinestone evening gown. She searched the bar before taking a step into it. I could tell she was having trouble with her contact lenses again. She looked like a concert pianist who had mislaid her piano.

'I wonder,' Tom said, watching her, 'what *she* writes?'

'Cheques, mostly,' I told him.

Karen's arrival altered something but it would be hard to say what. She blinked fetchingly.

'Hi! Am I overdressed?' she said. 'I don't feel in syntony with many of the people here.'

'You're not,' Tom told her. 'You're in syntony with the *bar*. You're the only one who is.'

Karen blinked. She didn't look convinced.

'This word. *Syntony*.' John said. 'Hasn't it something to do with radio receivers and electrical transmitters?'

'Oh I don't think so,' Karen said. She explained that it simply means when you're tuned into the people around you, like on the same wavelength as them, until she was interrupted by an outburst of raised voices coming from the group sitting in the window-recess. There followed the crash of a glass breaking and we all craned in the direction of the commotion. It looked as if some poets were throwing their drinks in each other's faces. They must have fallen out of syntony with each other. The word 'Stalinist!' was hurled. A man in a 'HANDS OFF NICARAGUA' t-shirt pointed his finger as if it were a loaded pistol at a light cotton David Bowie-looking suit and the man in it.

'. . . Fucking . . .'

'. . . Neo-Mannerist academic . . .'

'. . . Hippie Fascist . . .'

Bowie-Suit pushed the loaded pistol-like finger aside. He wasn't afraid of it. Then there was a scuffle during which Nicaragua T-Shirt threw a punch at Bowie-Suit they way you throw a stick for a dog.

'Oh no!' Tom groaned. He placed his drink on the top of the bar. 'The Bolinas Mafia are having a go at the Language Poets again!' He set off across the bar towards the brawl.

John leaned over and spoke in a loud whisper. 'Well now. Do you think it's meant to be like *this* . . .' he seriously asked us to consider '. . . on Parnassus?'

The fight ebbed out of the poets. For a while we couldn't speak or laugh, there was such a funny feeling in the air. Tom returned. We all somehow arrived at the decision that our dentures suddenly needed fixing.

Pudgy Fingers

In the suburbs, throughout the afternoon, brown-skinned immigrant construction workers in checkered shirts and with kerchiefs on their heads are the only people on the street, toiling in the sun, building walls, laying tiles, keeping out of trouble. There is nobody else around because the heat is too enormous and the shadow-line so sharp it leaves no margin for ambiguity, supports no secondary ecology, neither birds nor bicycles nor pedestrians. It could be the surface of Venus in the year 3000. The front lawns are perfectly maintained. The immaculate-looking flowering lawns probably conceal sonar security gadgetry. On the cement lip of the sidewalk a bullfrog squats, disguised as a brown speckled rock, except there are no other brown speckled rocks in the vicinity and it just looks like a dumb bullfrog. History has overtaken it. Ten years ago all this was farming country but the farmers have turned realtor. Why pick cotton when you can pick up a piece of boomtown? The bullfrog is looking for the cicadas that used to be everywhere here. Instead there is the cicadalike sound of a helicopter buzzing across the clear blue sky; it always seems to be up there whenever you look, plying the same course, like a fleck in the eye. All of a sudden an eight-cylinder Corvette Stingray roars off the slip-road, growls to a hault, deposits a pretty white girl in shorts who waves and skips quickly between the air-conditioning of the auto and the

air-conditioning of her father's house, crossing that dangerous intermediate zone. The moment she is safely inside, the
Stingray accelerates out of the turning-circle of the dead end
and disappears in the direction of the freeway, exploding
complex hydrocarbon molecules into simple oxydized der-
ivatives which it exhales into the atmosphere. The street is
silent again. The helicopter plies its course. A flattened
bullfrog sticks to the hot macadamized surface of the road like
a postage stamp.

It's like this wherever you go in the suburbs and almost
wherever you go in the city you will be in the suburbs, isolated
pockets of family-unit housing miles apart from each other
and linked by a web of freeways and telephone-cable through
which the wives and sisters are telling each other what they
bought down at the store. Each suburb is a five-minute drive
from an amenity zone where there is a bowling alley and a
hamburger bar and a supermarket in which the wives and
sisters can buy everything they need and some things they
don't need. These zones have names like Kerkwood, Oakleaf
and Piney Point Village – very rustic-sounding – and the
buildings there have the look of gas-stations, low pre-
fabricated shells that are dwarfed by the giant billboards that
advertise their existence, but none of them makes any claim
to being candidates for the Architects' Medal. There is even a
kind of honesty about their reason for being there: to make
a buck or two, no other. It is to these that the wives and sisters
come in their automobiles to cash the coupons they have cut
out of the local newspaper and buy commodities. In the
supermarkets they can find every brand of food produce:
twenty feet of colas . . . thirty yards of pet food . . . a quarter
of a mile of large uniform-sized fruit and vegetables. However, if they want something foreign or a bit fancy they will
have to drive a few miles more to the centre and do their
shopping in one of the larger galerias built on the rubble of the
decayed downtown of the Old City. Here there are entire
streets of stores in the same vast air-conditioned building that
is spacious enough for a 747 to turn around in. The streets
have glazed brick-tiled pavements and there are lamp-posts,
bars on corners, little chic boutiques selling connoisseur
products, whole areas given up to different themes: children's
requirements, women's business, sports goods, three or four

88

storeys linked by escalators. One half-storey is taken up by a plaza adorned with trees and fronted by fast food distribution outlets: Chinese Eats, Bar-B-Qs, Suzie's hamburger Palace, the Chelsea Pubb, Lenehan's Irish Bar, Alfredo's Pizza . . . This is where the kids come to drink soft drinks and eat each other's french fries and get themselves picked up. They seem to enjoy the ersatz atmosphere, the nylon garden furniture, the bubble-gum music piped through the air-conditioning. Well, it is the coolest place they don't have to pay to enter where something might happen. Here they can stroll around in short skirts, tight sexy clothes, while their mothers and sisters discuss their fathers and brothers over a coffee in the Old London Tea Room. Above all they can look cool; the temperature is always a pleasant fifty-five degrees. A uniformed security guard dressed to look like a cop plods the streets with his hands behind his back, says howdy to acquaintances, has a hamburger in McDonalds, just as if he were a real cop. Everything is just fine. The streets are clean and there is no traffic, there are no drunks, no frowning immigrants. Nobody seems to mind that there are no animals and you can't see the sky and it never seems to rain. Inside it's always three o'clock on a breezy California afternoon and you could almost forget that outside it's still Texas, ninety-nine degrees with a zero probability of precipitation – Houston, Space City.

To get from the house in Piney Point Village to the big shiny offices and hotels Downtown you have to ride the freeway –there is no other way of getting there. Many of the tall buildings Downtown have silver one-way mirror windows like Mr Cool's sun-shades; the shiny edifices are not required to give an account of their activities to passers-by. To get from one interior to another you can cross via one of the aerial tunnels linking the buildings of the business section. You can ascend to the rooftop heliport and take a 'copter or else descend to the internal parking lot and exit in an air-conditioned auto, reaching your destination without having left the controlled hermetic environment or having to encounter the heat, the bugs or the poor. In downtown Houston, going somewhere on foot and breathing ordinary air is getting to be something nice people don't do if they can help it; that's for the wretched of the earth – which is another reason for taking the car.

Once inside the silver hotels and offices it's so cool you need an extra sweatshirt and the tropical fish tank has a heating thermostat. Employees glide gracefully by, converse civilly, wishing each other a nice day. Carpets muffle all human footfall and an invisible tape output pipes nineteenth-century piano music played by a defected enemy virtuoso. The ambience is uncluttered; it has been washed by powerful office-cleaning equipment – insects with difficult Latin names and catalogued by Linnaeus have been vacuumed away. The bugs belong outside along with other stray organisms, microbes, heroin-addicts, olive-skinned knife-carriers, foreign bodies, criminals and communists. One characteristic of air-conditioning is that it only works effectively when doors and windows are well shut, but that also has the effect of making the realms of *within* and *without* symbolic categories; they not only are different places, they mean different things. *Within* is law-abiding and good, informed by the cool Rationalism that inspired the Declaration of Independence; *without* speaks for itself, wild and dangerous. They are the two conflicting interest groups that have made America the place it is; side by side, both ignore the presence of the other. There is no margin between these two worlds except the automatic opening and closing shatter-proof doors. From the temperate New England climate you step into a sweaty tropic; the lovely lovely people give way to people who are not so lovely and don't dress so smart. On the street is a different universe, cheap liquor stores, gun shops, the sign that reads 'ALL GIRLS TOTALLY NUDE' on the closed down clip-joint, the black man sprawled in the shade with a hand-written sign 'Please help me' which everybody ignores. A disparate citizenry of every complexion warily goes about its business; office girls out to lunch, young men with old eyes from over the border. All any of them has to do is step through the glass doors to become part of the American Dream. But air-conditioning is expensive, someone has paid for it, so the visitor who enjoys its benefits will eventually have to provide an explanation for his presence. Drift around for long enough and a young person will approach you and ask you with an airhostess smile if she can be of assistance. Over her shoulder on the wall are framed reproductions of Paul Klee and Braque, perhaps an original Henry Moore

90

bronze on a plinth. An overweight black private security guard lounges over his copy of the *Houston Gazette*, a Smith and Wesson .357 magnum in his holster. He isn't looking for trouble; the surveillance cameras are doing that. He's just there to frighten off the riff- raff.

I would get frissons of alienation hanging around those places, strolling through the foyers, riding the elevators, crossing inside the aerial tunnels. I was the guest of an oilman and his wife – a girlfriend of mine from years back – who had offices in one of these buildings. This gave me a pretext to roam them without having any business to. I also roamed the suburbs, where they lived, although I didn't need a pretext to do that. I needed my head examined.

Alan and Helen had a house in Oakleaf. Like all the houses in Oakleaf it was brand new; there were small signs that suggested the construction company had only just moved out: a pile of tiles . . . sewer piping . . . fresh-tilled earth. The backyards of all the properties possessed identical squares of coarse green grass that looked like Astroturf but was real enough. Sometimes through the kitchen window I saw the neighbours, Vietnamese and Indian families, who, Helen said, paid for their houses and cars with Welfare handouts; they pottered about their gardens but it was always too hot for me to try it. Of course, the immigrants and refugees shouldn't have been there in the first place – they brought the value of real estate down – and their success baffled people like Alan and Helen because they seemed to be able to make money faster than Americans could, which is pretty fast, and yet they didn't fit into the stereotype of spics and niggers. They were industrious law-abiding people. But they still weren't white.

'Imagine picking cotton in this heat,' I mentioned to Alan one time. The cotton fields had gone but the climate hadn't.

'They were used to it,' he said. 'They don't feel the heat like us.'

I knew whom Alan meant by 'They'; it was his inclusion of me in 'Us' that worried me.

Alan and Helen lived with two budgerigars and their son Davie. Davie was fifteen and he towered a good foot over my head and must have weighed two hundred pounds stripped. He had a big-boned smiling Scandinavian face with only Caucasian blood in it. They called him 'the Moose'. Davie's size was a subject the family never tired of returning to; it was a massive natural phenomenon, like a volcano which the surrounding villages are in awe of and in the shadow of which they make their daily rituals. It was always something understood that Davie would win a football scholarship to college. 'I've played enough football to know . . .' Alan told me occasionally – he was proud of his boy – '. . . and I've coached football teams. I *know* a football player when I see one. Davie's big and strong.'

But a funny thing happened while I was staying with Alan and Helen. They took me down to Davie's high school to watch the football team go through its first practice session of the season. We sat alone in the heat up in the vast brand new football stand watching the boys pumping and biffing and the Coach yelling encouragement – that furious sergeant-major abuse that is able to lift young men to feats. 'That's Davie . . .' Helen said, pointing to one of the identically padded and helmeted heroes. Mothers know their sons.

'That can't be him,' Alan said. 'The Moose doesn't play back. He's a front defensive blocker.' Then: 'There he is . . .' He picked out the largest boy on the field.

'Yes. That's him,' Helen said.

We watched Davie go through the practice session, weaving and blocking and standing with hands on hips listening to Coach. They all looked very dandyish, I thought, like sixteenth-century courtiers in their enormously padded doublets and their arses in tight little hoses, tiny feet in dainty leather slippers, prancing on the gridiron, though the temperature was in the eighties. When the boys trouped off after the session they were running in sweat, carrying their helmets. Some girls with long blonde hair and short skirts met their boyfriends and carried their helmets for them. 'Where's Davie?' Helen said. Suddenly he wasn't on the field. The player we had been watching turned out to be someone else. Alan stopped the Coach. 'Say, Coach, wasn't Davie in the work-out today?'

'Ah, Mr Erickson. Davie twisted his knee. I think he tore a cartilage. He's in the Clinic.'

Davie lay on a bed in the Clinic like a fallen idol. A girl in school colours was placing ice round his knee. He smiled grimly.

'Well, that's that,' Alan told Davie as he drove us all home. 'You won't be playing football for a long time – if ever. When a cartilage goes, there's no real mending it. We'll have to find another way to get you to college.'

I watched Davie hold back the big tear in his eye. And that was the end of Davie's football career – right there in front of me.

Something else Davie's injury put paid to was the planned hunting expedition up the Colorado River, but later that evening – while Davie sat in front of the TV with his leg strapped up – Alan showed me some of the armoury we would have taken.

'This is a regular twelve-bore,' he said. 'For birds we use it . . . And then there's this one, a real beauty, a .32 for larger game, deer . . . And this baby is a .22.'

'That's the one we kept loaded in the house when I was living alone up in Chicago,' Helen said.

'This is it. It would put a hole in a man, don't worry,' Alan said in his sensible way, as if I was worried. 'And this . . .' he lifted up another gun '. . . is an authentic Winchester Repeater.'

'The one they made the film about?'

'That's the baby.' He passed me the rifle to fondle. 'One of the most beautiful guns ever made.'

The way Alan cradled the guns they might have been a litter of puppies. I was nonplussed. Guns are always much weighter to hold, to be in the presence of, than they look on TV. To me all this calm discussion about rifling and calibration, the guns' potential for destruction, had an edge of obscenity to it. It was like ogling dirty photographs, depositing in the imagination unwanted fragments of violence and excitement. And it wasn't as if the guns were out of place; they fitted snugly into Alan's understanding of them. It was me, my mealy-mouthed attitude to the damned things, that shouldn't have been there.

That's the effect Houston has.

93

Alan liked to meet me early evenings for a drink in one of the big hotels, the Sheraton or the Hyatt Regency, which have the kind of bars where the waiters and bar-staff are dressed in the uniforms of First World War flying officers made out of a fabric that matches the wallpaper and the drapes. They were meant to have class, but as flunkeys they were offhand as hell; they had the manners of traffic police. The drinks tended to arrive in oversize goblets with a small iceberg floating in them and for the price they charged you could buy a bottle of the stuff at the discount liquor mart.

Alan and I were usually having an argument. I was what he called a liberal and he was what I would call an ultra-right conservative. Naturally that wasn't what we would have called ourselves. We hardly ever saw eye to eye on a single issue and we got along fine, enduring each other's company with politeness and good humour. Besides my old girl friend we had one thing in common: we liked each other.

We discussed what Alan liked to call the Race Question. He tried to open my eyes. He explained the matter carefully, adopting the informed tone of someone putting a person straight on a few facts. In his eyes I wasn't one of those subversive radical liberals; I was the plain ignorant sort.

'I'm not suggesting they are all out to knock you on the head and take your wallet,' he said in his quiet reasonable Mid West way. 'My point is they are, uh, endowed different than us. There are good niggers, sure. Our postman for one. But tell me one thing that was invented by an African. Go ahead, tell me.'

'The Watusi,' I said.

'You see, you can't. Seriously. There isn't one significant change they made to History. They don't have the same brain that we do. They are less advanced. It's a fact. Look at the levels of IQ in studies on black children.'

'Listen. Why do you need to rely on specious so-called facts you got out of *Plain Truth Magazine* for your opinions? Why not come out and admit you don't like black people? That's fine. There's no law says you have to.'

'We aren't talking about opinions. At athletic activities they can't be beat. They are faster than we are. Look at the records they hold at sprints. *That's* the reason they get into trouble so much. They have more muscle than sense. Look at the crime figures, if you don't believe me. Most street crime is committed by young black youths.'

'You telling me black kids had the same breaks as white kids?'

'Listen, let me tell you something. I went to an all-white school and if I had my way my son would go to one too. Now they bus all the kids to the same schools, since they desegregated them – worst thing they ever did. But there are still mainly black and mainly white schools. They built a brand-new school over in one of the black areas near us. It had a swimming pool, the best gymnasium, new classrooms. You know what they did? They wrecked it. In six months it was a wreck.'

I shrugged. Why should I give a damn what my old girl-friend's husband thought? It was spooky listening to the quiet reasonable voice talking such craziness in an emerald-upholstered facsimile of a bar, drinking something that called itself a beer, though that wasn't what I called it. Spooky because in that context Alan's point of view did not sound crazy; it sounded perfectly appropriate. *I* was the one who was crazy.

'Let's get out of here,' I said. 'I'll take you to a real bar.'

We got in Alan's car and I directed him the three or so blocks to Market Square, the heart of old Houston although all but two of the original two-storey brick buildings have been torn down to make way for parking lots and the back side of a supermarket. It was a melancholy place. Shady characters dozed in the shade under trees next to their bottles. Although Alan lived in Houston he had never set foot in Market Square. It was scruffy low-rent territory. But it has one of my candidates for the Best Bar in the World.

Inside the Carafe Bar it was as dark and cool as a country church, no air-conditioning here; you might even call it dingy. There were probably spiders in corners and other of God's creatures under the floor. Just a single customer was at the bar, a black guy sitting quietly at one end of it. We sat on stools in the middle and almost immediately another black guy came in and sat a little downaways from us. So there we were, bracketed between black guys. Alan and I couldn't think of anything to say to each other; it wasn't a good moment to carry on a debate about the intelligence levels of different ethnic groups.

95

I liked the Carafe because it wasn't brand-new; the bar had been built a hundred and thirty years before I got there, a brick and plaster long room that hadn't been renovated in any of the fashions of later periods. Inside and out, plaster had fallen away, revealing the narrow red-brick work. It originally served as a horse-changing station for the stagecoach, but today is still what it always was: a saloon. The charm of the place lies in the way it has been neglected, because it certainly is no museum. Behind the bar is a handsome carved set of shelves; behind that, an old dusty mirror. Scattered over the shelves is an unconnected collection of curios: an assortment of valise labels from all the best hotels in the world, a dust-covered pair of armadillos, stuffed and in mating position, an old pendulum clock that keeps good time and chimes on the hour. Over all this is a moose head that nobody shot in Texas. The bar top is a big unvarnished bench, or else the varnish was elbowed off it long ago, pitted with carved names. There is hardly an inch that isn't monickered by previous – and, it's to be presumed, mostly dead – drinkers. I had found it reassuring to drink in their company. Sitting in the same spot that Rocky Johnson and Jeff Gates had sat took the edge off drinking alone. In the Carafe you are never alone, you are another mortal in a long line. Others will drink here after you have gone, others after them. Like all really old places its survival gives a sense of continuance to the present. And, because it possesses the flavour of an era – signed as authentic – it requires you to pause and reflect on what has gone into the making of US America – Jeff Gates, Rocky Johnson. History, unvarnished, is under your fingertips, a refuge from the future that Houston is in such a hurry to inhabit.

We ordered beers and I read what had been written in chalk on a small blackboard at the far end of the bar.

Chapter 13

Foolishly attempting to retrieve his
cardboard box for profit, the old man
Biff is turned into a fuzzy creature
with four nostrils. And Adam. . . .

From where I was sitting that was as far as I could read. The barman shrugged when I looked at him. It meant nothing and had no reason for being there. Unlike the Hyatt Regency, the Carafe tolerated irrelevance and accidence, the dark side of causality that the Founding Fathers had refused to give admittance to when they invented the concept of America, but which ordinary people had brought along with them just the same. The Carafe was a bar for ordinary people.

The black guy at the far end of the bar broke the silence. Down the length of it he addressed the one who had come in last. Clearly they were acquainted with each other; they just hadn't felt the need to sit in each other's lap. Perhaps they both needed to savour a bit of space. He said: 'You hear about the bigot I picked up last week?'

The second black guy shook his head. 'How did you know he was a bigot?'

'Easy. He had pudgy fingers,' he said and then cackled. 'You can always tell a bigot by his pudgy fingers.'

Without thinking Alan and I spread our fingers on the bar and examined them for signs of pudginess and all of us smiled.

'Nope. It's okay guys. I already checked you fingers soon as you came in,' he said. 'You ain't no bigots.' He went on with his story and now we were part of the audience. 'Well, last Wednesday I picked up a fare right here in Downtown. He said he wanted me to take him to Rochester Avenue, over by the Astrodome. It was getting pretty late in the afternoon so I figured it would be quicker to take him direct down Alamo Street instead of round by the South Freeway. Soon as he realized I was going cross-town Pudgy Fingers says, "Hey, Boy, I don't want no guided tour. I got a meeting to get to." I says, "What kind of meeting would that be, Ku Klux Klan?" That gets him mad. "Listen nigger, never you worry what kind of meeting it is. Juss get me there tonight." I drives on awhile till we get to a quiet piece of street and I draws up. He says, "Why you stopping?" I leans down under my seat where I keep me a sawed-off for when I run into hoodlums. I turns round in the cab and I stick the thing right up Pudgy Fingers' nose. "Okay, Pudgy Fingers," I says. "This is where you and I part company." Then I cock the breech real slow and let him look down the barrel. He starts to look white then, even for a white bigot. "Yes, boss," I say. I jab the sawed-off an inch more up his nose until he says it: "Yes, boss," he says. Then I tell him: "Only reason I ain't giving you both these is 'cos it will make a bad mess of my cab. Now get you ass out of here." And he does. You never saw a bigot get out a cab more quicker.'

The cabbie took a bite of his beer and let us all think about that for a moment. Someone – maybe me – muttered: 'Holy shit!'

'But I d'nt finish with him yet. I leave him in the middle of nowhere and I drive round a couple of blocks and then I cruise up alongside him. He must think he's back in luck, finding a cab out there at that time of night. He hails me and I draws up a bit ahead of him. He climbs in and I says, "Where to, sir?" like a good nigger. He says, "Rochester Avenue," and I turns round and yessir him and give him my sweetest grin. He juss looked at me with his mouth open. You can believe me, he sat good and quiet till we got to the Astrodome.'

None of us moved. Over the barman's shoulder the two armadillos had paused in the middle of their mating, gripped like the rest of us. For a moment we were all flat, like figures in a daguerreotype, four drinkers and a barman – long dead – in an old dusty saloon.

As soon as we had finished our beers, Alan and I left the bar and rode good and quiet till we got to Oakleaf, drawing our different conclusions from the cabbie's tale. Alan – for the first time – didn't look happy. I knew he was thinking about his own collection of guns.

'Cheer up, Alan. Think on the bright side,' I said. 'Least we don't have pudgy fingers.'

Big Balls, Little Balls

It was a hottish Sunday afternoon and quiet in the old plaza, but not too hot or so quiet you didn't want to be there. Families in their best clothes sat on handkerchiefs under trees eating ice-creams slowly, as if they were enjoying them. Grandfathers with white moustaches played ball with grand-daughters, and teenaged girls in white dresses walked arm-in-arm around the flowering acacias that bordered the little fountain. In a darker part of the shade a group of brown-skinned young men wearing rolled cloth headbands were squatting in the earth, playing cards. (For the kids of New York rolled headbands are in fashion this year; for Navajos they have never been out.) But the young men weren't really playing cards; they were watching the girls without looking at them, the white of their dresses flashing unbearably as they moved in and out of the sunlight.

Hatless under the sun, a crazy stirred-up preacher-man in a three-piece suit who didn't look a bit crazy – he might have been a bank teller – was standing on a chair, punching a Bible while he harangued the scattered congregation in Spanish. He was giving them fair warning of an imminent disaster but nobody paid any attention to him. They seemed to know all about it already, the grandfathers and the granddaughters, the girls in white dresses, the brown-skinned young men. They knew what was coming and that it couldn't be averted.

Had it ever been?

El Paso was looking good that afternoon. It was hot all right but nobody was making a song and dance about it. People moved slowly, saluted each other gracefully, and a few large autos ghosted round the circumference of the plaza. It could have been the opening scene of an opera, the chorus in position, quiet before the protagonists have stepped onto the stage and the melodrama immanent in the place has started to unfold. On the fronts of the big Forties hotels the delicate tooled-leather ornamentation was restfully elaborate for eyes wearied by the bathroom-tile proportions of American cities; there were quoins and cornices and lintels. The smaller hotels off the plaza had dusty antique neon signs on them, moulded at a time when neon had been the latest thing, which nobody since had been able to afford to replace. The few people visible on the streets moved as if they had a right to be there, leisurely – none of them was hurrying to work – their gait expressing an invisible element of the place. The women particularly looked good, tall Mexican women dressed with flounce, mysterious after the unmysterious short skirts and pointy tits of American girls. Even the cops looked good in their gallon hats and high-heeled leather boots and silver-inlaid revolvers – long-barrelled pistols like toy Colt .45s, not the stubby Smith and Wesson sort that shoot people. But best of all was the sense of complexity. There was a subtlety to the form that events took which could not be grasped at first glance. Here there were ambiguous penumbras. Acacias and falling water. Eyes looking out of the freckled shade of woven straw hat-brims. The Rio Grande and the poverty of Juarez on the other side of it. High sierras in the distance. There was the long established truce between two different peoples living side by side, the romanticism of a cause well and truly lost but never forgotten.

I found me one of the cheap Forties hotels. The unlit green neon sign outside read 'GARDENER HOTEL' and inside there was an empty marble and stucco foyer at the end of which I paid my eleven dollars in advance to a man who needed a shave even more than I did. He gave me the key to Room 13 and told me not to worry, nobody had died in it yet. I rode an old brass-worked elevator up to the first floor and took a look at the room. It was just a room but I had to peek behind the drawn blind to see if there were any suspicious characters hanging around below.

I showered and shaved and lay on the bed smoking a cigarette. Then I put on some cotton clothes and dug out my pair of white naval officer's shoes; I thought El Paso deserved them. If I had been wearing a moustache I would have combed it in the mirror. It was Sunday. I wanted to look my best. I had a date with a bottle of tequila in the Folded Sails Cocktail Bar.

Between a short-order restaurant advertising 'Breakfast All Day' – 99 cents – and a tiny cinema showing a movie called *Alvidrez Diseño Sanguino*, the Folded Sails carried on its business behind smoked glass doors. Stepping through them into the air-conditioning, I got the impression that the same people were sitting on the same stools as when I had left the place an hour or so before, quiet Americans in white panama stetsons – except for the one who was sitting on what I already affectionately thought of as my stool. I climbed onto the one next to it and put my hat on the bar. Everyone else, I noticed, kept their hats on their heads.

The bar itself was a small square, cutting down the distance the barkeep had to walk, an arrangement which gave the place an intimacy and made room for a pool-table in back. The young Mexican woman behind it let me have her Aztec smile on the house and said: 'Same?' She made me feel like an old customer.

I watched her take a martini glass from the fridge, rub the rim with lime, twirl it in a saucer of salt and place it on a paper napkin in front of me. Into a shaker she poured a slug of tequila, a splash of curaçao, a double splash of orange juice. She didn't so much shake the stuff as wave it around in the air. Then she strained the drink from the ice into the glass, exactly the quantity to fill it until there was no room for any more. The whole business took about forty-five seconds. I resisted the temptation to make a grab for it and let it lie there for a moment, trading smiles with the Aztec. Country and Western music was coming from the juke box:

. . . I've got rid of the pillows
   Where she used to lay her head,
I've picked up her hatpins and curlers
That she dropped on her side of the bed.
But where can I put her memory
   When it haunts me night and day?
I can't hide it in the closet
   And Lord I can't throw it away . . .

I could do this all afternoon, sip sunrises until the sun set. Sooner or later, however, the American on the stool next to me goes: 'What kind of time do you have, friend?'

'I have Central Time,' I go. 'What about you?'

Examining his wristwatch, he goes: 'Me, I'm still on Pacific Time. Say, sir . . .' He turns to the old feller on the other side of him. 'Are you folks on Mountain Time here?'

'We're on El Paso Time,' the old feller growls without looking at him. This is one of those parts of the USA where life is carried on in the present historic.

Turning back to me the American says: 'I'm from San Francisco, me. Waiting for a bus to Louisiana,' as if answering a question someone has just asked him. I stopped myself looking over my shoulder to see who it was. Then he did it again: 'I got to catch the eight o'clock to San Antone. Don't want to miss it.'

I felt obliged to reciprocate his disclosure in exact proportion. 'I've just come from Louisiana. On my way to San Francisco.' Adding for friendliness' sake: 'So it looks as if we're meeting each other halfway.'

'El Paso's halfway to anywhere you want to go,' he aphorized. The man on the stool next to him moved his head almost imperceptibly. I held my breath but nothing happened. Until, suddenly, a hand jabbed out at me. 'I'm Steve! Howdy!'

I said howdy and gave him my hand and let him shake it up and down as much as he wanted. I told him my name, but no more.

Steve was about the same age as me, so there would be things we had in common, like Del Shannon and the Cuba Crisis. Like me he was kicking his heels, waiting for a bus, drinking in a bar. We were two people passing through life in opposite directions, each heading for the place the other had just left. I had to admit there was a certain symmetry to the situation, a kind of balance. He was even sitting on my stool.

'I just broke with my Old Lady, right?' he said. 'After five years we broke. Broke my heart too, damn near. S'why I'm going home. I'm from N'Orleans, you know that?'

'No. I didn't.'

'Yeah. I'm catching the eight o'clock to San Antone. I just couldn't stay in the same State as her no more. You know, me and my Old Lady – my ex-Old Lady, I should say – we had some good times where you're going. Beautiful place, California. You want to swim? You want girls? You want the best climate in the world . . . ?'

What could I say?

'. . . I'm going to miss near ever thing about that place. I'm going to miss my Old Lady too. My ex-Old Lady, I should say.'

I couldn't say anything – any minute I was going to start talking about *my* Old Lady – so I dug out a pack of cigarettes. When I proffered it to Steve he grinned. 'Ain't you a bit young to be smoking these?' he said.

I looked at him.

'These days it's only old-timers you ever see smoking Luckies.'

'Well if you *see* them, means they're still alive.'

'What the hell!' He took the pack and hooked out a cigarette. 'You either smoke or you don't.'

It was then, as he took the cigarette, that I noticed the three fingers missing from his left hand, the three middle fingers, which meant his thumb only had a little finger to play with. I didn't have to ask to find out why.

'I lost these . . .' he held the lighted cigarette where the missing fingers should have been, between his thumb and his pinkie '. . . in a shooting incident. My partner didn't know what he was doing. My ex-partner, I should say.' Then: 'Let's us have a beer!'

He ordered a pitcher of beer and we talked some more on the subject of California, the fine weather you get up there. Beaches. Mountains. Wine. The girls. Are there girls anywhere else in the world like Californian girls? I told him probably not. He said definitely not.

'What about you?' he asked suddenly. 'What's *your* story?'

'Oh, you know . . .' I procrastinated.

'No. C'mon. Where you headed?'

Rashly I said: 'Alice Springs. It's in Australia.'

'I know where it is. What takes you there?'

'I have a rendezvous with someone,' I told him and, in order to completely level the balance: 'My Old Lady. I'm going round the world one way, she's going round it the other. We aim to meet up on the other side of it.'

Steve made a puzzled face. 'How come you ain't travelling together? A man and his Old Lady should always travel together.'

'We can't.' I wanted to leave it at that but it was too late. 'My Old Lady isn't like me. In fact, she's completely different.'

'I don't get it,' Steve said.

'Well, she's a woman to start with. Men and women have to travel in opposite directions if they want to get somewhere together,' I said. 'Like electricity.'

'Don't that mean you're always saying goodbye?'

'Means you're always meeting up with each other.'

'Sounds kinda lonely to me.'

'Without the loneliness it would be meaningless,' I bullshitted. Well, he asked for it. It was one of those conversations between strangers in a bar, killing time, shooting the breeze, buying each other drinks. Keeping the balance.

We were drinking beer now, a pitcher between the two of us and out of glasses from the fridge which gave an edge to the stuff. It was four o'clock in the afternoon – El Paso Time – and one of us had to get on the San Antone bus in four hours. The other had nothing better to do than keep him company.

Steve said: 'Last time I was in El Paso, right? – years ago – I went 'cross to Juarez with my partner. We got drunk and rolled around Juarez in a beat-up Plymouth looking for whores. Man, were we drunk! Somehow we got into a fight and they called the cops. It was the old Mexican stand-off. The cops didn't know whether to jump in and get their uniforms dirtied up – my partner was a fighting kind of man. In the end we got in their car and let them put us in jail for the night and the next day they took us to the border and pushed us into the Plymouth and told us not to come back. I never been back too. Man, we had a bunch of laughs in Juarez . . .'

It was like the words of a rock 'n' roll song rendered into prose. I could almost remember which one.

'How 'bout a smoke?' he said without any preamble. 'I have a joint of good grass here.' He tapped his breast pocket.

Well, there it was, the intimate invitation – just like that – after the balanced introductions, precisely that casually offered risk which you like to think you are adept at eluding, the suggestion that the boundary of acquaintance be enlarged beyond the confines of mere bar talk. In situations like this the difficult thing is not just that the shift between the status of strangers to that of buddies is so sudden – which it is – but that the shift is imperceptible; it has no ritual expression, no contours for your judgment to gain purchase in. It's like having to change gear in a car that has automatic transmission; instinctively your foot hits the clutch pedal, only there is no clutch pedal – just an accelerator and a brake.

What the hell. You either smoke or you don't.

'Right. I'll go to the john,' he said. 'I'll leave it on a tile some place over the wash-basin. You wait a moment when I get back, then go for it.'

I nodded. And that's what happened. I sat and watched my cigarette burn and the time disappear before everything went funny. When Steve returned I went to the john and took my pull on the reefer. By the time I returned he had moved our drinks from the bar and was laying the balls into the frame on the pool table. Already I was beginning to lose any influence over the direction events were taking.

I told Steve I had never played pool in my life.

'Relax. Watch me and you'll learn.'

On the table the white cue ball rested on the spot, solitary in the face of the odds stacked against it, the solid phalanx of colours, striped and spotted, at the opposite end of the baize. I knew exactly how it felt. Very soon the nice symmetry in the situation would be shattered, not by chance but as a consequence of what Steve and I would do. Our colliding fates.

In pool the idea is that you pot all the balls – stripes and spots – except the black one. If you pot the black you're dead. It's easy, so long as you don't make any mistakes; those you do make you have to pay for. Before you are allowed to pot the black there is an ever-changing situation compounded of chance and causality. The whole business is full of hidden meaning. Well, after a reefer and a couple of pitchers of beer it is.

Steve didn't tell me the rules, he left me to pick them up as we went along, something you can only do by losing. But he did give me two pieces of advice: 'The way I play pool, you tell your partner what you aim to do, which ball you're going for and into which pocket.' And: 'Always take the most difficult shot first. That way you leave the easy ones until last.'

'The pink in the far pocket,' I said over my cue, lining up the shot . . .

'Man, you'd never believe how many hours I spent inside pool rooms,' Steve said, chalking his cue. 'I played pool since I could lift one of these. Where I came from it's what you did. There wasn't nothing else.'

. . . the white careered towards the pink, struck it at an angle, thereby altering its own course and setting the pink in the direction of the far pocket. The pink dropped nicely into it just before the white ricocheted off the cushion, against a dead ball and into the middle pocket.

Steve put down the chalk. 'I get a free shot,' he said and told me which ball he intended to go for. I noticed how neatly the cue fitted into the gap between the little finger and thumb on his left hand where the fingers were missing, as if playing pool was what his hand had been designed for. After the difficult shots he took the easy ones until there were hardly any balls left on the table. Then he let me have his third piece of advice: 'When you can't do anything else, stymie your partner.'

Playing pool with Steve was like talking to a lawyer. One moment everything was simple and the next it was all snarled up. My errors became his strategy. The white went where I sent it but for most of the time I had no idea where to send it and so I made mistakes. My intentions didn't seem to have much bearing on the game. And yet whatever happened it was my fault.

It made you think. Especially the way the black lurked around throughout the game, avoided, always close.

After the third game, which Steve, by some brilliant play, allowed me to win, we ordered another pitcher of beer. There was plenty of time left before he had to go for his bus. We were still holding the cues, wondering whether to play another game, drinking the beer, when two men came across the bar towards us. They were big Texan fellows and they were both wearing some kind of uniform.

'You boys mind if we play a game of pool?' one of the two men said.

I didn't mind. Steve said: 'You better ask my partner. He just beat me.'

So we were partners now.

'He must be pretty good, huh?' the second man said to Steve.

'Mind if we play?' the first said to me with what sounded like respect.

'Go right ahead. I can't play anyway,' I said.

They grinned at each other, at my patently false modesty. One of them said: 'We can't play either.' And the other: 'Fact, I bet we can't play more than you can't.'

'I bet you a pitcher of beer,' Steve said.

They grinned at us and we grinned at them. While one of the two men was putting his quarter into the slot, Steve handed me the frame and told me to break and then disappeared into the john. I did the best I could. I broke and, as luck would have it, got rid of some of the balls. When he came back he asked me whether they had been spots or stripes.

'Spots,' I guessed.

'No, no. You have stripes. Big balls,' one of our opponents corrected. '*We* have little balls.'

After Steve had sunk a couple of stripes they introduced themselves. 'I'm Nick. This is Rad.'

We shook hands, said howdy, gave our names.

'Where you boys headed?'

'Florida,' Steve lied. I didn't say anything, allowing them to think we were on our way to Florida together. A pair of buddies. Like them. 'Catching a bus to San Antone tonight.'

'Travelling Trailways?'

'Matterofact we're going Greyhound.'

'Greyhound? Phaw!'

'Y'see, we're Trailways drivers.'

'You should travel Trailways. We need your support!' Nick said.

'Trailways drivers have little balls, Greyhound travellers have big balls!' Rad said, sinking another spot.

'No, no. *We* have big balls, *they* have little balls!'

It was getting hard to remember what kind of balls any of us had. Luckily someone at the bar watching the game told us: 'Trailways has spots, Greyhound stripes.'

My partner threw me a look only a partner could have gotten away with. He took a couple of difficult shots. I couldn't see any easy ones. As our position deteriorated his shots became increasingly desperate.

'Look what he's going for, Rad! This man's crazy!'

'I don't know who plays a crazier game of pool,' Rad said to me. 'You or him.'

'Steve taught me everything I know,' I said.

Rad and Nick whipped us five games straight.

'You boys weren't kidding. You *are* worse than us!'

'They're terrible!' Rad, sliding his cue into the rack, said. 'you know, I'm sorry. We're going to have say goodbye to you two fellers. We got buses to drive.'

'You going to Flagstaff, we'll give you a ride. Leave at midnight.'

Steve looked across to me. I could see he was seriously mulling the offer over. And we were, after all, partners.

'How 'bout a smoke before you go?' he said.

'You got some grass?'

For a moment the two bus-drivers pretended to consider the proposition. Then they headed for their hats.

'It sure has been a pleasure playing with you,' Rad said while he settled his cap comfortably onto the crown of his head.

'And don't forget now,' Nick said over his shoulder. 'You travel Trailways next time!'

The bus-drivers left the bar and we returned to our stools and looked at the fresh pitcher of beer which had just been bought for us. I couldn't recall why. Everything was back to front. Spots and stripes, I was beginning to see them everywhere I looked.

'Well, we killed the time,' I said. It was just coming up to a quarter to eight.

'We murdered the mother!' Steve said.

It became clear we were not going to be able to finish the pitcher tonight. I left a dollar bill on the bar for the Aztec and collected my hat and my partner's hat. I had a duty, it seemed to me, to put him on his bus even if he didn't seem to care about it himself one way or the other. We steered each other towards and through the smoked glass doors, out of the air-conditioning into the thin desert air. It was nice and cool. The sun had gone down and there were people on the street. Cool-looking people.

There is no way of knowing what time of day it is in a Greyhound Bus Station. White panelled-in strip lighting beams onto in-transit passengers trying to get comfortable on shamrock green moulded-plastic chairs, specifically engin-eered, along with the lighting, to prevent them from succeed-ing. Blacks, Philippinos, Hispanics, an Amish couple, the carless, the homeless, the mad, wait without expecting anything, placid like animals on which ingenious behaviourist experiments are about to be performed, shadowless under the white lighting, without the penumbra of cause and effect that normally etch people into the complexity of their background. Nobody is reading. Nobody is speaking to anyone. One or two are familiar from other Greyhound bus stations in other cities – the man whose portable TV you helped him with in Baton Rouge, asleep on it, the children you amused on the bus, in their mother's arms, lovers in each other's.

Seven fifty-four.

The second hand of the big clock on the wall was slowly flaying the passengers – clunk, clunk, clunk – who had to sit tight and take it until it reached the point at which it would be time for them to pick up their possessions and get on with their lives.

Seven fifty-five.

'Let's go take a quick smoke!' Steve said. He dove into the men's restroom without giving me time to reply. I decided not to follow him. I had my balance to keep. I just waited, like everyone else.

At one end of the waiting area a woman in chocolate-brown uniform with primrose piping waited to serve pre-cooked hamburgers and fries on matching brown and primrose poly-styrene platters. Facing the gates, a cop sat in a perspex booth waiting to come off shift, glancing up to make sure there were

111

no bag women or hobos, violators of State laws or Company policy.

Brown in the far pocket, blue in the side.

Over the speaker a polite voice requested passengers holding tickets for San Antonio . . . Austin . . . Houston . . . and connecting destinations to please make a line at Gate Number Three. And thank you for Going Greyhound.

Seven fifty-six.

The passengers in front of Gate Number Three were already filing through, handing their tickets to the driver. I went to dig Steve out of the men's restroom. I knocked on the shut doors and called out to Steve to hurry it up because the bus to San Antone was about to leave. A row of young Mexican men, lounging and murmuring as if the restroom was some kind of bar, watched me in the mirror. There was no reply from behind any of the doors so I looked under them. There was no one called Steve anywhere.

I got back to Gate Number Three just as it was being shut. The clock showed one minute after eight. The driver would be straightening his reversing mirror, reciting Federal and State regulations to the passengers. I couldn't see what else I could do. Steve wasn't in the restroom and he wasn't on the bus. I felt cheated because I had not discharged my duty to put him safely on his way. I had lost my partner. That or my partner had lost me.

Sober, I walked away from the situation, back to the Gardener Hotel across the empty plaza, now cool and completely silent except for the tinkling of the little fountain. The white dresses and the cloth headbands had disappeared, along with the stirred-up preacher man who probably had to get up early for his job at the bank. Now it was just a quiet plaza in the middle of an American-Mexican town at nightfall. Trees and the shadows of trees.

But – the more I thought it over – Steve had told me what he had intended to do, to get the eight o'clock San Antonio bus. The San Antonio bus had left without him. At the last minute there must have been a more difficult shot he had to take first. I didn't know what it was. I didn't care.

One thing was for sure, if he hadn't been able to do anything else, at least he had stymied his partner.

His ex-partner, I should say.

People Who Like Maps

A hard rain is driving against the windshield faster than the wipers can shift it, so hard and fast I have to turn off the freeway, even though Dallas, which is as far as I'm going, is only a half-hour away. The light's fading. The car in front has its tail lights on even though it's only three o'clock in the afternoon. We're both crawling at thirteen miles per hour. When it signals to turn into the rest-stop exit I follow suit, even though this one is a Stukeley's. Most of the vehicles do the same. Only the truckers keep going, but with them it's a matter of principle, a question of style. Aside from anything else, they would never be caught dead in a Stukeley's.

As I drift right the big trucks slowly accelerate past me in the fast lane. It's a bit scary, you have to admit. Just a mile back you passed four wrecks slewed across the emergency lane, ambulance lights flashing, wet-faced policemen in big yellow PVC slickers waving you to keep moving, bawling silent oaths at you as if it was none of your damn business what was going on behind them: ambulance personnel winching out the slumped motionless bodies from the wrecks.

The cheerful DJ on the Dallas radio station is loving it. Every ten minutes he hands you over to the Weatherman for a report on the 'sityation': '. . . remember that raincloud I talked about? Well, it just dumped a half-inch of rain on Royce City in the last twenny minutes! And it's heading for

115

the Metroplex. That's what I said. It's going to be here momentarily. Half a inch, huh? That'd be a lot of water for November. For August it's one helluva lot! Ooooeeee! How ya'll doing, you folks in Royce? Good time to wash the dog I guess . . . Now I had no idea now many people suffered. Silently. From serious scalp problems – psoriasis, eczema, dermatitis – until Nutrogena asked me to mention their new T-Jell product. And now – my goodness! – everyday's mail includes letters from grateful users . . .'

Before you know it the News has merged into an advertisement, the truth into fiction. You have abandoned your car. You are standing in Stukeley's Roadside Restaurant ready to buy something.

Stukeley's is doing business. The car park is full of cars. The customers – all soaked just from running from the cars to the restaurant – are exchanging exclamations of wonder and disbelief. I take an empty stool at the counter and wait with my back to it for the waitress to come and take my order.

Lightning flashes.

The waitress squeaks. She isn't in a hurry to take orders. Like everyone else she's staring at the rain. 'I never saw anything like *this* before!' she says. The feller on the stool next to me says to her: 'Well *I* did! This is a Florida monsoon! Maybe it's one that lost its way.'

The other waitress, the white-haired one going round with the jug to freshen up customers' cups of coffee, stands with her mouth open, holding the jug, gazing out of the windows at the rain. You can't blame her. Everyone else is doing the same. In fact, standing there in her orange uniform, holding the jug, hand on her hip, she sums it up. This is something else. We're all in this together. Stuck inside a Stukeley's during The Flood.

Lightning flashes again.

Did you see that! I don't believe it! Y'know, I'd juss hate to be struck down by lightning!

'That's where I'm going,' the feller on the stool next to me goes. 'Florida. Be lucky if I make it to Royce!'

I look at him because I'm the one he's speaking to. I can tell he's a man who doesn't expect people to disagree with him. He has a round waxy face, unshaven, without any colour in it. Come to think of it he looks a bit like Jack Ruby in an old black and white TV clip.

116

'It won't last, I guess,' I lie.

'It won't huh? Where ya heading?'

'Dallas.'

'Pfaw! You're on home plate! Me, I have to get to Tampa, Florida! I guess you're on business.'

He's a man who likes to know your business.

'Yeah. In a way,' I admit guardedly. I'm someone who doesn't like telling people my business, especially people I meet in roadside restaurants.

'You got to have business in Dallas or you're just wasting your time . . .'

The waitress – she's standing across the counter in front of me with her pad and ballpoint at the ready like a traffic cop booking me for a violation – says: 'Okay. Now what's it going to be?'

'I'll have a beef sandwich,' I tell her.

'Thing else? Sidesaladfries . . . ?'

'With horseradish.'

'*Wha-aat*?' The waitress screws her face up from all the pain she's experiencing trying to understand my enunciation. 'Horse Dish?'

'Horseradish.'

'What in God's name is that?'

'Something people put on beef sandwiches.'

'I never heard of it,' she says. She folds away her pad. There isn't anything else to say. She hasn't heard of it.

'. . . yeah. Like I was saying. Bars, restaurants, strip-joints,' Jack Ruby continues. 'Dallas has the lot. You'll hate them all. Downtown Dallas is dead. *Dead*! And suburban Dallas, well it was never alive. How d'you like bunny rabbits?'

It sounds to me like a trick question so I say: 'They're okay.'

'Then you gonna love the city buses! They're painted to look like Bugs Bunny. Pink. With whiskers. And ears!' He sticks up two fingers each side of his head and wiggles them. 'The only thing in Dallas worth a good goddam is Solly Soloman's Turf Bar on Commerce Street. You drink, right?'

He's a man who likes to ask trick questions.

'Solly Soloman is the only guy in Dallas who'll give you the time of day. A friend to a thousand luckless souls. Take me.' He taps his chest. 'For one.'

117

'So what's this Turf Bar got,' I ask him. I have to ask him something. 'That makes it special?'

'Nothing,' he says. 'Nothing special 'bout the place 't all. It's a dump. A dive. All it's got is a old wood bar and plastic stools with strips of black 'lectric tape stuck where they split. And beer company signs to light the place. All you gonna find at Sol's is old drunks, hustlers, oddballs. Sol never kicked no one out. Even cops drink at the Turf but they never made a pinch there yet, that I know of. It's got what all them new Yurpean wine parlours with ferns and lady waiters don't got: *Sleaze!*'

He delivers the word with a dash of verve, as if it has the same meaning, the same timbre, as a word like *Style*.

The waitress, on the move, deals me a plate off the arm and keeps moving. I open the sandwich and take out the slices of pickled cucumber and squirt what might be mustard onto the beef from the yellow refillable rubber bottle. Then I tear open and empty the sachet of non-dairy creamer into my coffee. On the reverse side of the sachet, I notice, it says: 'Use of this product may be hazardous to your health. This product contains ingredients which have been determined to cause death by cancer in laboratory animals.' I take a bite out of the sandwich and then a mouthful of coffee, listening to Jack Ruby. But all the while I'm wondering in what respects I'm supposed to be different from a laboratory animal.

'There's a lot of people in Texas like to call themselves Christians. You seen them yourself. They're the turkeys driving around in Mercedes and Lincoln Town Landaus. They should pay a visit to the Turf Bar any night an' count how many times old Soloman sticks his fist in his pocket for some down-an'-outer.' Jack Ruby laughs in a way that isn't particularly infectious but I can't help liking him. 'They'd only try an' get a Sanitation Order slapped on the place. It ain't the sin they object to, mind. Nor even the virtue. It's the *Sleaze!*'

'I'll see if I can pay it a visit,' I say. But I'm wondering whether it isn't about time I went back to being a vegetarian.

'Yeah. Pay Sol a visit. Tell him it was me sent you. Munger's the name. Mort Munger.'

Mort Munger borrows the waitress's ballpoint and, on the reverse side of a paper napkin, draws how to get to the Turf Bar. He draws carefully, writing out the names of the streets. He's a man who likes to draw maps. 'This is Commerce, right?

118

it's one way. Right here between Hotel Adolphus and Neiman Marcus is a row of old buildings. You can't miss 'em. They're the ones without aluminium and smoked glass windows. *There's* Sol's Turf Bar . . .' He marks the napkin with a cross like a pirate's map.

'Thanks,' I say and I take the napkin and fold it carefully in my wallet, next to my MasterCard to show him how much I treasure it.

As soon as the rain eases off Mort Munger punches me softly on the arm, says, 'So long pal,' and heads for Tampa, Florida. I head for Irving, which is a suburb between Dallas and Fort Worth. I'm delivering a brand new chocolate-brown-and-cream Mercury Marquis stationwagon from a carmart in Philadelphia to its owner, a man called Randy Starr in the Raxell Computers Headquarters. It's his new company car.

The tall symmetrically planed surfaces of Dallas take shape in the cloudy distance like a crystal formation in a solution. I'm driving Mr Starr's new Marquis along Interstate 30. After a few miles of suburbs, Interstate 30 hits the Lyndon B. Johnson Freeway circle and becomes the Thornton Freeway. Suddenly there are about ten lanes all going different places. Signs direct you to Mesquite and Buckner Boulevard and White Rock Lake. I keep my eyes on the car in front. It's a black Porsche. DOWNTOWN. DO NOT PASS. Down a ramp, up a ramp. THIS LANE MUST TURN LEFT. I tail the Porsche. At the side of the road, just under the exit of the Northwest Highway Ramp, there's a police car in the emergency lane. I turn my head to see what's going on.

Framed in the nearside-door window, a black woman is lying on the tarmac with her arms straight and her head to one side. She's wearing a white blouse, a black skirt, her hair curled. She's middle-aged. Tidy. Someone's mother. Dead. I see all this just before the police officer covers her with a black plastic sheet that looks like a torn plastic trash bag.

I turn my head back to the car in front. The Porsche is a bit too near and I have to brake. I'm touched by the policeman's solicitude. There are no wrecks around so my guess is she jumped off the Northwest Highway Bridge. I find myself

119

wondering whether she knew she was going to do this when she put on her white blouse and black skirt this morning, when she put in her curlers last night. The business of choosing which clothes to die in seems more poignant than the body lying beside the freeway.

I draw alongside the black Porsche. For a moment we are travelling at exactly the same speed, parallel. We both follow the arrow for Downtown traffic. I notice that the Porsche has some sort of bodice over the front lights and radiator grille, in matching black leatherette with velcro fasteners for quick release. I've never seen anything like it – automobile lingerie! – and I can't help smiling.

The blonde-haired woman behind the wheel throws me a look and catches me smiling. She thinks I'm fender flirting, smiling at *her*, and gives me a friendly grin. I transfer my allegiance from the leatherette bikini on the car to the blonde-haired woman driving it without a qualm.

The sun is shining on Dallas through breaks in the clouds, its beams reflected onto the wet asphalt off the glass-sided walls of the First Chemical and Federal Reserve banks. I cruise the length of Harwood, past the Scottish Rite Temple and the Masonic Temple and the First Presbyterian Church. You can't help noticing that there is no shortage of places to pray in Dallas. Or to keep your money. The First Chemical must be one of the names by which He is known.

The Bradford on Houston Street, the flophouse in which I was planning to spend the night, hasn't been demolished. It has been refurbished into a classy five-star hotel. The polite Iranian bell captain in maroon and gold-lace uniform tells me that this is on account of it being the only hotel on Houston. Word has gotten round that you can see the exact spot where President Kennedy was assassinated if you stick your neck out far enough from certain east-facing windows. The bell captain shrugs apologetically.

It's on the bell captain's advice that I take Spur 35e to the Stemmons Freeway for the Dallas-Fort Worth Airport strip where the less expensive motels are, the Delux and the Ramada and the Howard Johnson. The lanes are crowded with homeward-bound white office-workers in Fords and Toyotas. Every vehicle contains a single driver, no passengers. We are all overtaking each other in the fast lane or the slow lane, in fact wherever the opportunity exists. There are no rules. I guess that's why it's called a freeway. You see an opening and you go for it. It's expected of you, if you want to get ahead. While I'm wondering about the kind of lives the white office workers lead I miss my exit: Spur 482. I don't like the sound of Loop 87 and before I know it I'm heading out of town on Interstate 77.

The rain decides to come on hard again now. The light is fading too but this is because evening is drawing in. I pull off the freeway into a Chevron gas station which is brightly lit and looks friendly and I park in the lot over by the pay telephone booths. I turn the air-conditioning off and the radio on. It's the man in the Weather Bureau giving the latest report on the 'sityation': 'High winds and heavy rain are currently hitting the Dallas metropolitan area,' he tells us. He doesn't have to tell me. The stuff he's talking about is swirling in curtains across the lot, smacking against the sides of the Mercury. '. . . a man was killed earlier this afternoon and several buildings damaged in an industrial stretch of Northwest Dallas . . .'

A beige Rabbit draws up alongside the Mercury and a young woman in a white cotton summer dress gets out and flits across to the telephone booths. The pay phone booths are virtually open so she's wet to the skin by the time she has punched out her number.

'. . . Jo Silverman, aged sixty-eight, was killed by a lightning bolt while running from the Seven Eleven store on Manana Drive, Irving, to his pick-up with his groceries . . .'

The woman in the booth turns round so that the telephone cord winds itself across her body and she mouths words to the man sitting in the Rabbit behind the wheel. Her dress is so wet now that you can see the white of her lingerie underneath it. One of the curtains of rain lifts the blue plastic garbage bins from under the pumps and, tumbling it over and over, carries it across the lot. Over and over it goes. The paper towels inside are being strewn in all directions. The gas station attendant runs out into the rain, holding onto his hat, to retrieve the bin while I listen to the radio. Madonna is singing

121

one of her disco-tease songs: '*Get into the groove, yeah, you gotta prove your love to meeee . . . !*'

The gas attendant's red baseball cap is blown off his head. He leaves the garbage bin and runs after his hat. Lightning is cracking all around us – enemy artillery trying to get our range – lighting up the whole of Irving. I want to tell the gas attendant to forget the damn cap. It's not worth it. I can't help thinking about Joe Silverman struck down carrying his groceries from the 7-Eleven to his pick-up.

And the white blouse and black skirt of the middle-aged black woman on the Thornton Freeway.

And J. F. Kennedy.

The young woman – she has replaced the telephone onto its cradle – walks back to the Rabbit. Slowly. She doesn't care how much wetter she gets. It doesn't look as if the news is good. I can't work out whether she's crying or it's just the rain. Inside the car she puts her hands up to her face in a gesture of despair. I wonder if she's related to the late Joe Silverman. The driver turns on the lights and backs the car out of the space.

I switch off the radio and punch the cigarette lighter to ignite. While I'm waiting for the lighter to warm up I ask myself whether it would make any difference if I believed in God. Or at least had a lot of money.

I settle for the Ponca Motel. It's the only motel in a short shopping strip that looks a lot newer than it. There's a McDonalds, a Shoney's, a Long John Silver Seafood Restaurant. No surprises. But the purple and vermilion neon Red Indian in profile with 1950s Cadillac tailfin head-dress and the sapphirine lettering of 'PONCA MOTEL' should be in the Museum of Modern Art, 'COLOR TV WITH RADIO $14.48. VACANCY'. The single-storey cabins make a U-shape around a swimming pool. The only cars outside any of them are a brand new Cutlass estate and a black Porsche.

I check in and park the Marquis outside Room 19. It's turned into a nice night. The big yellow M of the giant McDonalds sign is reflected on the surface of the swimming pool, chopped into pieces by the blue water. The rain has disappeared for good. You can still see the last of the clouds rolling like molten boulders towards Oklahoma, revealing a deep gentian night here and – over there where it's still evening – a stormy sunset backlighting the raised freeway of the horizon and the red white and blue Mobil Self Service electric sign on stilts.

I can hear the TV in the next cabin. The place is virtually empty and they put you next to an occupied cabin.

The first thing anyone does in a motel room is to switch on the TV. The second is to try the shower and then take one. The third is to pour a drink and lie on the bed and watch the TV. I do these things in the traditional order. Then I put through a call to Mr Randy Starr on his private number. He says hello and I explain who I am. 'I have your new car, Mr Starr,' I tell him.

'Oh,' he says. 'What kind of car is it?'

'It's a Ford Mercury Marquis stationwagon.'

'Is it a nice car?' he asks me.

I can't bring myself to tell him the truth. It's a slug. The handbook warns you against driving it over eighty-five. 'Sure. It's a very nice car.'

'What colour is it? Is it blue?'

'No sir.'

'But I asked for a *blue* car!'

'I'm sorry. It's chocolate and beige brown.'

'Oh no!' he sobs.

He tells me to drop it off at his place of work tomorrow. This is my last night with Mr Starr's new slug.

I watch a movie on Channel 20 which has Kirk Douglas playing an obsessed military scientist who is trying to get even with the Government for firing him. He breaks into a missile silo which is meant to be impregnable and aims the turkey at the Soviet Union. The only person Kirk will deal with is the President who – to avoid a World War – allows himself to be taken hostage and both men are shot down in a hail of fire from Army sharpshooters under the direction of Richard Widmark. Without warning advertisements flit across the screen, haunting the action of the movie. It takes an effort to tell which is which.

I dress and kill the TV, open the cabin door and lock it after me. While I'm doing this the woman in the next cabin is doing the same. We look at each other and she smiles at me. She's

123

dressed all in black – black slacks, a black embroidered bolero-type vest over a black shirt. It makes her face look very white in the half-light.

'Hi!' she says, still smiling.

'Hi!' I say. 'Is that your Porsche?'

'Yeah. Do you like it?'

'It's very nice. I especially like the little leather bikini-thing it's wearing.'

'I think it's cute too. I live up in Colorado. It can get cold there nights.'

We cross the carpark together, skirting the swimming pool.

'Looks like you're heading the same place I am,' she says.

'Looks like everyone is,' I say.

Across the pool a family is pouring out of two adjacent cabins. There are about six kids, all sizes – neat, excited, well-behaved – and Dad in an open sport shirt, blue shorts, white knee-length socks. They're Mexicans. Dad is a Chicano who has made it. He owns a brand new Cutlass estate. He's shepherding his family towards McDonalds as a treat because they have been stuck inside all day on account of the rain. He's carrying the smallest, in his arms. At the one way street that divides the motel from the McDonalds the kids wait, hopping and screaming for Dad to catch up and say they can cross.

We follow the family in, stand in line together.

'What are you going to have?' she asks me.

'Quarterpounder and fries,' I tell her.

'Yeah. Me too.'

I take my tray and sit down and she follows me and sits down opposite me.

'Okay if I join you? I need to talk to someone. I just watched a movie on TV that made me want to throw up.'

'Did it have Kirk Douglas in it as a mad scientist?'

She has freckles.

'Oh you saw it too. Yeah. It's the kind of movie they like to show in Dallas.'

She has neat short fair hair. Neat nails. Neat teeth. She's neat. Everything about her.

We talk and eat. Her name is Odette. She's a systems analyst for a Denver computer manufacturer. A Ph.D. She's thirty-three. We finish our quarterpounders and conversation

124

at about the same time, touch up our mouths with the paper napkins simultaneously.

'We seem . . .' I say.

'We seem to be . . .' she says.

We both laugh.

'We seem to be in sync, is what I was going to say,' I say.

'Okay. Well. If we are – what next?' she says. She champs her neat teeth. 'I could murder a beer!'

One of the Mexican kids, the smallest, a three-or-four-year-old girl – comes right up to me and stares into my face. Over her head her dad, mouthful of hamburger, gives me a wink of encouragement. The little girl grabs hold of my thigh which comes level with the top of her head and stares up into my eyes.

'I guess you made a hit,' Odette tells me. 'Where shall we go?'

'Well, if its *sleaze* you're looking for . . .' I take out my wallet and unwrap the paper napkin from around my MasterCard, spreading it out on the table between us. 'X marks the spot,' I tell her.

We study the map for a while. I tell her what Mort Munger told me. Eventually she says: 'It has to beat the Sheraton bar or one of those places.'

I take hold of the little Mexican girl's hands and kiss one of them gallantly. 'Farewell, my lovely,' I tell her. She gives me an old-fashioned soft-focus up-from-under kind of look – Veronica Lake in the last reel – and Odette says: 'Hey! C'mon! Don't break her heart!'

We decide to take the Porsche. Obviously. I'm standing outside the passenger-door waiting for Odette to unlock it for me. Over the top of the car she says: 'D'you want to drive?'

'You trust me?'

She shrugs. 'I trust men whom children trust,' she says.

Whom. She said *whom*! A Ph.D with freckles.

Getting into a Porsche isn't like getting into any other car. It's more like getting back into the womb. Snug. Responsive. Exciting. You slide in under the wheel and suddenly everything is at hand. It's an hermetic environment in which your comfort is a coefficient of its function.

Odette takes off the sunroof and then I back the car out of the lot and edge it gingerly towards the raised freeway, taking

125

my time. I don't want to get there too quickly. When I oversteer clumsily Odette murmurs: 'Easy.'

'I never drove one of these before,' I explain.

'You mean, one that responds like this? You'll get used to it. Just be gentle. Don't forget, you've been rolling a barrel around all your life.'

I sneak along the slow lane of the Stemmons Freeway, tooling the engine in second until there's a gap in the Mercedes and Lincoln Town Landaus ahead and then I hit the gas.

'Oh boy!'

I'm slammed back into the sheepskin.

'*What*!'

The coloured lights of the gas stations and eateries blur into white.

'*Wow*!'

Our hair stands on end.

'*Aaah*!'

Then the parachute opens and we're straining against the safety harness, entering the triple underpass at the start of the Dallas-Fort Worth turnpike.

'Well . . . ? Did the earth move for you?' Odette asks me after she's let me give her a ride in her own Porsche.

'Does it go faster if you take its bikini off?' I ask her.

She grins. 'Oh sure! That was quite a *modest* performance.'

As soon as we come out of the underpass we cross Houston and we're Downtown. I fish out the paper napkin from my pocket and hand Mr Munger's map to Odette. 'Y'know. I've always liked people who like maps,' I tell her.

'I know what you mean,' she tells me. And I know she does.

It's a good map. Two blocks past the Hilton we recognize the row of old buildings on Commerce – gunstores, sex-mag bars, liquormarts, the natural habitat of your Downtown sleaze. The Turf Bar is well camouflaged against it like a rare critter, almost extinct. We have to cruise Commerce a couple of times before we locate it.

The street is almost deserted. We pull over outside the bar. It looks quiet. The Michelob and Lone Star beer signs are unlit. There's a heavy steel grille padlocked across the gateway and, affixed to the grille, a sheet of paper with felt-tip words written on it. A message.

126

We both get out to take a closer look.

The message says: 'OWING TO THE DEATH OF SOL SOLOMAN THE TURF BAR WILL BE CLOSED FOR THREE DAYS AS A MARK OF RESPECT.'

Neither of us knows what to say. Odette shakes her head, murmurs: 'Oh Dallas!'

We get back into the car. She takes over the driving seat, without thinking, and sparks the engine. 'Well, so much for sleaze,' she says, looking over her shoulder before pulling out. 'Let's go sneer at the Sheraton.'

Totaled

The light in Phoenix when the sun goes down is heart-rending – the peaceful expression on the face of someone dying in his own sweet time. Fragments of neon vermilion, shocking pink, violet azure, are reflected in the windows of the tall commercial buildings rising out of the decay of old Downtown, gilding their ugliness exquisitely. Glimpsed between them, on the horizon, is the nuclear fission of a desert sunset, after which everything will be different. It's a moment of metamorphosis that sends shivers down the spine. The attractive young executive men and women have vacated the cool banks and offices. Having nosed the VW Rabbit into the flow of Lincolns, Buick Mk IVs, Sedan de Ville Cadillacs, they are already back in their wooden houses in the residential suburbs, loosening neckties, taking cans of Bud Lite out of the fridge, turning on the TV ready for the ballgame. The cheerful delis and boutiques servicing them are all shut. The heart of the city is empty. Almost the only vehicles on the streets are taxis and police patrol cars. Imperceptibly, as the light changes through the violet end of the spectrum, the place of the daytime busyness is taken by less glamourous activity. Soon, after the sun has disappeared completely, the elegant deco-arcaded sidewalks will be haunted almost exclusively by shuffling shadowy groups – Apaches lurching from one bar to the next. And, occasionally, by tall white cops in pressed navy blue cotton uniforms, cautious, handsome, slowly getting in and out of their cars.

I was on my way from the Golden West Hotel – a ten-dollar-a-bed flophouse where the man on Reception really was unshaven, wore a string vest and had a limp – a rare species that is becoming extinct as its habitat, the old Downtown hotel, disappears. There's no key to room ten, he said, limping ahead of me down the corridor. You'll have to ask me to open up when you come in. Or who's here. We're here twenty-four hours. I said, Don't worry. It's fine. The taxi-driver who dumped me there had warned me what to expect. It stinks, he said. I asked him, What's the best bar in town? He said, Depends the sort of place you're looking for. Me, I go for Bee Jay's. They have good music and it's all brand new. It's clean. Bee Jay's didn't sound like the sort of place I was looking for. I had had enough of clean bars. So I asked him, So what's the worst? That's got to be Lil's over on Monroe, two blocks south from the Golden West. You can expect to get knifed there for sure. It's where the drunks and trash all go. Indians. Whores. It stinks, he said.

I was on my way to Lil's over on Monroe just as the sun was going down, enjoying the clean warm air after the fetid chill of room number ten, admiring the light.

I was careful to give a wide berth to the clumps of Indians swaying down the colonnaded sidewalks, clinging to each other to become a single many-legged organism, human rafts adrift on the asphalt symmetry. It so happened that two of these rafts converged on each other from opposite directions just as I was about to edge around both of them, at the very moment they decided to cohere into a single body. I had the impression that none of them could see me – they were nearly all blind drunk – and seemed only aware of each other, but this may have been a mistake. I found myself hard-shouldered out of the way, from a harmless drunken lurch or by way of a warning, a final twitch of fight left in the last indigenous warrior people to be subdued by the US Army. Either way it hurt.

Apaches have the look of Apaches. They have oval Apache faces, Apache eyes, stocky Apache stature. They dress with a bizarre inconsequentiality that is nevertheless Apache. They hold on to each other as if they are not a lot of separate people

132

but are part of the same person, one who knows that 90% of them are going to die of alcohol-related diseases.

And still – after dark in Phoenix – there's something that's not quite right about them. Or else about Phoenix. After dark they take over the heart of this hot modern city not as if they had a right to it but *as if it weren't there!* As if all the polished white marble and aluminium framed mirror-glass in the world couldn't obliterate the fact that this place, under it all, belonged to *them*. Ghosts returning to their territory. In the fading light it wasn't the Apaches' right to be there which seemed to be the issue, but that of Phoenix.

Lil's Convention Bar leant against a level tract of empty land that was waiting to be built on. Battered, a funky survivor, it looked about the busiest spot in town. Because it was next to Lil's the vacant tract was probably impossible to sell, a realtor's nightmare. I eased myself past the bunch of Indians loitering around the door and went inside, found an empty stool and sat on it. Nobody tried to knife me. The big blonde bartender came up and took my order. Bourbon on the rocks, beer to back. A dollar 75. Thanks. You're welcome. She was wearing a t-shirt with words on it: 'BE NICE OR YOU DON'T GET NO GOODIES.' I didn't look too closely at it. I didn't look closely at anything except myself sipping beer in the mirror. There was plenty going on but none of it was any of my business.

Down the far end of the bar the TV was relaying the ballgame. The bases must have been loaded because the pitcher kept looking over his shoulder before his unwind to see if the man on first was going to try and steal second base.

It was one of those very long bars – about twenty-five bar-stools, most of them occupied, three pool tables in a line. There were also tables where groups of men and women sat, played poker-dice, ribbed each other, drank. The place was quietly going wild. Feeling loosened up, I ordered another pair of drinks and swiveled my stool around and leaned my elbows against the padded rim of the bar so that I could take in the pool game that was in progress as well as the rest of the action. On the juke box Fats Waller was singing. *'Ain't misbehavin'. Savin' all my love for you.'*

It was the most mixed clientele you ever saw together in the same bar: plenty Indians, some blacks, a few whites, the odd Chicano. And various women. Over by the door there was a

133

paraplegic white feller in a wheelchair, his head lolling, a can of Bud in his lap, spilling over his pants. But he didn't look like a wino. He was shaved. Across the floor Apache women danced with each other, giggling. There was a young casually dressed white guy with neat moustache, Adidas tennis shirt, arms around the waist of a fat middle-aged Indian woman. It didn't look right somehow, two people from completely different ends of the economic pile although it was none of my business. When a drunken Indian approached the woman to dance with him, Adidas Tennis Shirt told him to get lost. The woman got up and danced with him anyway. Adidas Tennis Shirt grinned sourly. It was like this all over the place, trouble storing itself up for later. The kiss of pool balls. Laughter surging, subsiding. Appreciative noises from the guys with nothing better to do than watch the baseball. *'Ain't misbehavin'.'*

On my right side there was a black man in smart casual clothes who also had his elbows on the bar, watching the dancers. He wore a tie and a shirt with a button-down collar, leather slip-on shoes with white socks. A dude. He was drinking 7-Up. We made brief eye contact and nodded to each other but that was as far as it went. He looked clean and shy and I wondered if he was out for a pick-up. His hair was cropped short the way you don't often see black guys wear it these days.

You got a cigarette? the woman on the other side of me goes. I proffered her one from my pack and lit it for her. She took the pack out of my hand as if she had never seen one like it before. It wasn't a brand she would normally have got from the bar cigarette machine so she guessed I bought them some other place. Where you from? she said. New York? I nodded to make things easier for myself. What about you? She said, I'm from the Reservation. What's your name? I gave her my name and she told me hers: Anita. You going to buy me a drink?

What would you like?

What you're drinking.

I ordered bourbon on the rocks with beer to back from the bartender. A dollar 75. Thanks. You're welcome.

Want to dance with me?

No thanks. I don't dance well. Tell me what's it like on the Reservation?

134

Anita shrugged. She wore her hair shorter than most of the other Indians I had seen. She was still young enough not to have lost her figure or her teeth. Perhaps she was even as old as twenty-five. I don't know whether she was pretty but she was attractive, in spite of the thin scar along her neck, following the line of her jawbone. She laid a hand on my knee. My family's land is on the Reservation, she said. They lease it to white folks.

Why . . . ?

Because they're dumb I guess.

The fingers of her hand began walking their way up my jeans towards my crotch, spider-like, as if they had a will of their own. I lifted them off just in time and carefully returned them to their owner.

I mean, why don't your family work it themselves? I said. She said, If they want to grow corn in the desert, let them. We may be dumb Indians but we ain't that dumb. She hadn't let me let go of her hand, I couldn't help noticing. It was nestling in hers on her lap. I disengaged it in order to light myself a cigarette. Or maybe the other way around. What are you, she said. A fag or what?

Across the floor – under the framed oil painting reproduction of Apaches galloping into the sunset, hair blowing, Winchesters raised – Adidas Tennis Shirt was getting stirred up. The Apache woman he had been pawing was still dancing with the Drunk. They were getting it on. '*Jumping Jack Flash.*' They looked as if they were made for each other. Adidas Tennis Shirt, however, didn't think so. He went over and peeled the Drunk away from the woman. The woman didn't seem to care one way or the other but the Drunk wanted to talk things over. Adidas Tennis Shirt ignored him until he realized the Drunk was not going to lay off. He stopped dancing, picked up the Indian and carried him to the bar and lowered him onto a stool and put a handful of coins on the bar-top. He was laughing now. '*It's a gas gas gas . . . .*'

It won't cost you your wallet, the woman called Anita said. If that's what's worrying you.

Over at the table nearest to the door the paraplegic white guy was doing his darnedest to wheel his chair to the door. It was painful to watch the heavy weather he was making of it, his nerveless fingers working to get some kind of purchase on the smooth rim of the handwheel. There was no way of knowing which was giving him more problems, his multiple disabilities or the effects of the alcohol. His head lolled and rolled with the effort. It was heroic, the ratio of the progress he was making to the effort he was putting into it. He had covered half the distance to the door when a foxy young black woman marched down the length of the bar – she was holding a pool cue in her hand – and took hold of the chair, swung it round and parked it at the table it had set out from. The three old Indians already at the table drinking beer watched, expressionless. She leaned over and spoke to the paraplegic, laughed in his ear and readjusted the beer can in his hand. Then she hurried back to the pool table. She was wearing pink lip-gloss and matching cotton pants and a sheer blouse that you could see her bra through. It was her shot.

Take my advice. Stay clear of these here women, the Black Dude next to me said just loud enough for me to hear. It's not worth it. I looked at him but he wasn't looking at me. He was watching the Fox lining up her shot on the other side of the pool table, her blouse opening as she leant over. She kept glancing over her shoulder to make sure her man in the wheelchair wasn't thinking of having another crack at stealing a base.

Lil's Convention Bar – as far as I could see – lived up to the boast painted over the door outside: 'The Most Unusual Bar In The West'. The intricately moulded plaster ceiling, the assortment of junk on the walls, the variety of humanity the place embraced, was out of kilter with the sprawling tidiness of Phoenix, the shadowless surfaces of the office-buildings selling computer systems technology, of the banks amassing the profits from the sale of them, designed – along with the passé futurist furniture inside them – for people who never fart.

The taxidriver had been right: Lil's was for the trash, men and women who drank alcohol in order to get drunk. And to forget. But the things they most wanted to forget were staring them in the face. There were two paintings on the wall, the one of the Apaches riding into the sunset – Winchesters aloft, glorious – and another, over by the paraplegic, of a huge naked white woman, blonde, of a certain age – she looked like the President's wife – with breasts of such vast proportions that the artist had been forced to shorten the legs considerably in order to fit them into the canvas. These two optimistic depictions of reality were a counter-weight to the business which was actually being transacted: whores and clients, mostly Indian, mostly drunk, dancing, dice-playing, playing pool. On the juke-box someone was singing *'Don't send me no doctor. He'll just give me a pill'*. I caught the bartender's eye and she refilled my glasses without a word. *'Just send for Dr Feelgood. He knows where I'm ill.'*

The paraplegic feller had set out again on the Great Trek from the table to the door, like a reptile to the water-hole, as if the survival of his species depended on it. I watched his clumsy fumbling out of the corner of my eye. Turning the wheelchair through 180 degrees had not been easy. Now he was inching the vehicle onwards in another pathetic bid for freedom. Anita indicated her glass to the bartender, who looked across to me, who shrugged and nodded. The paraplegic's keeper, the Fox, as soon as she saw he was up to his tricks again, left off her pool game, turned him around, and shoved him back where he belonged. She wasn't laughing any more. In fact she looked as if she was about ready to lash him to the table.

Why d'you want to know about the Reservation?

I don't know what a Reservation is, I said.

She said, Nothing to know. It's a piece of dirt white folks don't have no use for. She slapped my knee. 'bout the only place you can't buy a McDonalds!

I don't get it. Why particular people need particular lands *reserved* for them.

The Reservation's where the Government wants us to live. Or die. She ran the tip of her forefinger along the fine line of her scar as if it were a border between important events in her life and she were reminding herself where it was. God made the White Man and God made the Apache, she said. And the Apache has as much right to the country as the White Man.

I didn't try to argue with that.

On the other side of the bar Adidas Tennis Shirt wanted his woman to leave with him – they were back sitting down – but she wasn't having any of it. She was having too good a time. *'Oh Nadine! Is that you?'* Maybe she didn't feel like being his woman after all. The way she looked at him, laughing into his

137

face, he could have been just anyone. Drunk. Swinging her hips. The way a man hates a woman to look when he means business. I couldn't figure why a well-off young white man would want to go with her anyway, a woman with a kindly old face, old enough to be his auntie. '*Oh Nadine! Is that you? Seems every time I see you you got somen't else to do.*'

What's a sweetheart like you doing in a dump like this? The only reason a white guy comes in here is to find him a Indian woman, Anita said. She took hold of my hand. Thanks for the drinks, she said. I said, You're welcome. She let go of my hand and siddled away from the bar. *Oh Nadine!*

There was a small explosive smack. Had Adidas Tennis Shirt struck Apache Woman? Or she him? It was hard to tell. Laughing, she didn't seem to care if he had. Nobody did. From the roar going up down the far end of the bar, in front of the TV, I guessed it was a good strike from the hitter for the Phoenix Giants. Two three to count, with nobody on, he hit a high-flyer into the stand. Round the third, he was headed for home. Yeah, you guessed it, some brown-eyed handsome man.

The paraplegic finally made it out of the door. The Black Dude in white socks and I exchanged glances. The paraplegic's foxy minder was standing in the doorway, cussing the hell out of him. She banged her pool cue on the floor a few times. But she let him go. That's how she would get back at him. It was just a technical question whether a drunken white paraplegic in a wheelchair was more at risk in downtown Phoenix at night than he would be in the charge of a young black fox out for kicks who hated him. I looked again at the Black Dude but he had turned his back on the tableau. He had begun playing with a gizmo, a hand-sized two-way radio, listening to its crackle. The place was going crazy. It was a moment primed with violence, sex and fear. Something had to give. The bases were loaded. '*Oh baby, don't leave me here all alone.*'

The Fox stormed back through the bar, her evening ruined, and ran up against an Apache woman who was standing in her way. The Apache Woman started talking to her, gesturing in the direction of the door. Before she finished what she had to say the Fox slapped her three or four times, very quickly, across the face. The Apache – it was Anita – did her best to defend herself with her hands. Then the Fox cracked her once with the thick end of her pool cue. Anita went down holding her head.

I stood up but the Black Dude barred my way, shoving an arm across my body. Adidas Tennis Shirt's Apache Woman was helping Anita, holding her in her arms, but there was blood coming out of her face. Half the bar was wondering which side it was on, the other half couldn't care less. The TV continued to flash the ballgame. On the juke-box someone was singing something about going home. Something – a glass ashtray – flew across the room and ricocheted off the head of the Fox and she also went down. So the Indians hadn't lost the art of throwing things. It was time to get out, just the moment two officers from the Arizona State Police Department – tall, handsome, white – decided to pay the place a visit.

The officers hove through the door with the lazy lumbering gait of athletes, meeting the gaze of anyone who looked their way, unabashed, as if they were the guests for whom the party was being thrown.

The Black Dude had taken the floor. He was holding a plastic wallet with a metal badge inside high over his head, exactly how detectives do on TV. Nobody seemed surprised. Not even me. For some time now I had had the feeling I had a walk-on part in a made-for-TV movie. Hokay folks. Take it easy. He spoke to everyone in the bar, his back to me and the bartender. Ain't going to be no trouble. The uniformed cops didn't say a word. Their Magnums were in their holsters. The black one must have made a gesture I couldn't see because they went straight over to where the Fox was sitting on a bench, holding her head. One of the cops examined her head carefully, like a nurse. Then they helped her to her feet and led her out of the bar as if she was an old woman they were helping across the road. The black cop in the buttoned-down collar said something to Anita. She shook her head without looking at him and then he followed the others out of the bar.

I turned my back to the bar – the show was over – in order to drink my beer. The juke box was playing Marvin Gaye and Tammy Tirrell singing '*I've got your picture on my wall. But it can't sing or come to me when I call. Your name.*' In the mirror over my shoulder one of the pool players was leaning over his cue, lining up his shot. '*It's just a picture in a frame.*' There was the crack of pool balls colliding against each other. The player moved round the table. Anita was sitting alone over on one of the foam benches, not looking at anything. In front of her was the glass of something Adidas Tennis Shirt's Apache Woman had bought her, untouched. *'Ooooh baby. Don't you know? Ain't nothing like the real thing.'*

'BE NICE OR ELSE' cruised by, said, How you doing? Time to quit, I told her. She nodded as if this was a wise move. I collected my dollars from the bar except two which I left on it for her. Thanks. Thank *you*. You're welcome. Take it easy.

A patrol car was parked outside but the blue light wasn't flashing. The black detective was leaning into it, speaking into the radio. The woman – she didn't look quite so foxy now – wasn't in the car so I guessed they weren't arresting her. She was speaking to one of the cops who was writing in a book. The other cop was standing behind the wheelchair in which the paraplegic was flopped like a heap of old washing. I dunno. He looks pretty totaled to me, the cop said. How d'he get like this? He'll be fine in a while, she said. Believe me. I know him. Yeah? *'Oh no. There ain't nothing like the real thing, baby.'* He'll be okay. I dunno. *'Ain't nothing like the real thing.'* Okay. Yeah. Well. Take it easy.

Pink Lips

After the flat grain-farming country and the silver grain silos aimed at Russia, the small towns tucked into folds in the landscape and four-cornered corrugated-iron farm-buildings. Then the billboards for Shoneys, for 7-Eleven Realty, for Alamo Water Beds – 'IF YOU AIN'T SLEEPING ON WATER YOU OUGHTA!' – and for the Living Pentecostal Church of Christ – 'BEWARE THE HIGH COST OF LOW LIVING' – and the beautifully proportioned white water towers, each with the name of the small town it waters painted in bold letters on the side: . . . COOKESVILLE . . . LEBANON . . . ROCKWOOD. After the gas-stations the towns, after the towns the gas-stations – the gas-station attendants chasing the dirt out of the shade into the sun all day with long-handled straw brooms. Only after the radio is turned off, the car parked, locked, the deal struck between the polite young woman on the motel desk and the MasterCard Company, only then the cold shower and the opportunity to get some sleep.

But the radio is still on in your head: '. . . highs in the nineties. Some slight chance of thunder tomorrow. It's ninety-eight degrees out on Metro Airport and ninety-six here on WSM FM, Nashville ninety-five FM . . .' The air-conditioning fan is humming along with Merle Haggard: '*Rolling with the flow, goin' where the lonely go – Anywhere the lights are low. Sleep won't hardly come. Where there's*

143

loneliness all around. But I've got to keep go-o-ing. Travellin'
down this lonesome road – Rollin' with the flow. Goin' where
the lonely go . . .'

You sleep, dream, wake up, turn the radio on, take another
shower, sit wrapped in the motel towel at the too-small
writing-desk watching the TV without the sound. On it
there's a man pointing at a row of Perdue's yellow corn-fed
chickens in a supermarket – the women shoppers picking out
the chickens they want to buy as if the man gesturing to them
is invisible. You'd think they'd notice, especially as this – you
don't need the sound to tell you – is Mr Perdue himself
explaining why he eats his own chickens and if you buy one
and don't think it's the best darned chicken you ever ate well
you can come back to him and he'll give you your money
back.

'. . . good to see Texas Rangers getting back on the
winning track. They've won four of their last five games after
their All Star break last night. Texas play Cleveland once
again tonight in Arlington . . .'

There's a six o'clock shadow on the light coming in through
the primrose-coloured drapes, bathing the leather-bound
book on the too-small writing-desk in a kind of shadowy
primrose colour. You open and flip through the book, then
run your finger down the index of mental states travellers fall
prey to together with the pertinent references to the sections
in the main text for their assuagement. You can't find the one
that fits although there is a whole long list to choose from:
Loss of Faith. After a Broken Covenant. Before Death.
Temptation to Intemperance. Despair. Thoughts of
Suicide . . . In the end you let the book open where the silk
marker already is: 'How fair and how pleasant art thou, O
love,' you read. 'Thy stature is like to a vine and thy breasts to
clusters of grapes. I said, I will go up to the vine, I will take
hold of the boughs thereof, now also thy breasts shall be as
clusters of the vine, the roof of thy mouth like the best wine
that goes down sweetly . . .'

'Amen,' you go. You close the book and turn up the sound
of the TV. Eventually you put on a pair of jeans and open the
door, step out and look at the motel parking lot. You see half
a dozen good medium-priced American cars, including your
own, a white Cadillac Seville with a piece of fluttering paper

144

spiked to the radio aerial. Barefoot, you go take a look what it is. The air feels good and warm after the AC chill of the room, Mr Perdue's corn-fed chickens, the list of states of mind – the gravel hot underfoot. What it is is a napkin with 'HEY YOU PARKED TOO CLOSE' written in blue ballpen. This must be a joke or something. If the creamy Oldsmobile sedan parked too close to the driving side of the Seville was where it is now when you arrived you would not have been able to get out of the car except through the passenger's door. You can't help standing there shaking your head, although you try not to look too baffled in case you're on *Candid Camera*.

The motel – a Continental Inn – sounds as though it might belong to one of the big national motel companies. On the other side of the glass walls of the Check-In foyer you can see the profile behind the desk of the polite young woman who checked you in. She's watching TV, the colours of the picture reflecting off the surface of her face and making her blonde hair flicker. The glass door is locked. You realize she can't see you so you tap on the glass until she looks round. As soon as she does you wave. She makes a friendly gesture of recognition with her finger and smiles.

'Hi!' the tinny little speaker level with your ear goes. 'Everything okay?'

'Everything's fine,' you go into the little tin microphone level with your mouth. 'I wanted to ask if you could telephone a taxi for me.'

'Sure . . . Why not?'

You can't think of any reasons.

'You know you coulda phoned me straight through from your room to do that?' she says.

'Oh, I felt like stretching my legs,' you go. The glass door clicks and you push it open and enter.

'Where you want this taxi to go?' she says. Leaning back in her chair, she makes you feel more important than the movie she's watching on TV. 'Sometimes they like to know.'

'No particular place. I was going to ask the driver if he knew somewhere . . .'

'This your first time in Nashville?'

'Yes,' you tell her.

She watches you wonder whether she's going to take pity

145

on you. 'Okay,' she says. She grins. 'I'll get you a taxi. It'll be 'bout ten minutes. You're in room twenny-seven right?'

'Right.'

'This bar I'm taking you . . .' the taxidriver informs you. 'Is in Vanderbilt, opposite the University. I think you'll like it. I never saw any students in it personally. They all too Godfearin'.' He's a big man with a small moustache like a circus liontamer. Friendly. He gives you a free tour of Musicland. 'See that ol' cabin there? That's Studio B where Elvis cut "Heartbreak Hotel". 'Fore he took up with Colonel Parker and started playing shit. Most of this is tourist shit. Elvis Wax Museum stuff. See Hank Williams' house . . . ?' He waves a circus strongman's arm out of the window at a low Tennessee-style country house with beaten bars – the crotcheted and quavered kind – in front of the windows. 'They moved it here a couple of years back, brick by brick from where it was.'

'Where was it?' you ask him.

'Oh, I dunno. Some place like Maplewood . . .' Then: 'I'm a songwriter m'self, y'know that? I just drive this . . .' he beats the top of the steering wheel with the palm of his hands '. . . to make the scratch to demo some my songs. It's a hard town to try and be a musician in, Nashville! I should be in the religious literature business!'

He lets you out in front of a row of one-storey stores. You can only tell which of them is the bar by the Miller beer sign in the window. He waves the change out of $5 at you. 'Maybe I'll see you later,' he says. 'If you're still around.' He drives back up Broadway.

The bar the taxidriver says you'll like is a long hall with a small counter in back, a lot of tables and chairs, scruffy, with out-of-date posters for rock gigs on the walls and a couple of poker-game machines. An ancient Miss America pinball table. You stake out a spot at the counter and order an iced Guinness. Already it looks as if the taxidriver was right.

Four men and the bartender are leaning with their backs to the TV, joshing a feller in Duck Head bib overalls who is playing darts with a girl who could be either his wife or his daughter.

146

She's getting a lot of encouragement from the men which she doesn't need because, as one of them puts it, she's pissing on ice. After she beats him there's a kind of lull. You can hear the words of the movie on the TV behind the bar. It's a black and white movie about a white couple and their – if not black, not exactly white – baby. The dartplayer in bib overalls takes the stool next to yours and the girl goes behind the counter and draws him a shell of beer and one for herself. Still grinning, he hands her two dollars. The man facing you diagonally across the bar is cleaning his ear with a miniature tuning fork. Over his head, on the TV, a youngish-looking future President of the United States and a pretty blonde woman – perhaps, in the movie, his wife – are gazing down at a baby chimpanzee in a crib. The chimp is wearing white lace baby clothes. 'Well, honey,' the future President is telling her. 'We're just going to have to try and find a way . . .'

At that moment the front entrance door crashes open. You – you all – look round. A man with a Zapata moustache, in gas-station attendant's coveralls, clumps – there's something the matter with one of his legs – towards the bar. 'Will y'all take a look what the man gave me!' he hollers. 'Said t' feed y'all!' He's carrying a family-sized to-go pizza box in two hands. The box is placed on the counter and opened, the hot mozzarella cheese steaming, sticking to the lid. Smells good. Hot salami! Oh boy! Broccoli! Holy shit!

'Okay, hands off!' the girl barkeep goes. 'You want I serve it out Willy?'

'Go 'head! Serve it out!' Willy says.

The pizza has already been cut into eight equal segments. The girl barkeep counts heads, then separates the segments with a knife – there are exactly eight people in the bar – and hands a slice to everyone on a napkin. She says to you: 'Would you like t'eat some pizza?' You nod greedily.

'Broccoli! Did you ever see broccoli on a pizza before?'

'You complaining! How many *free* pizzas did you see?'

'Man it's hot!'

You have a hot broccoli pizza party, washed down with ice-cold Guinness. Oh boy! Holy shit!

'The Cont'nental . . . ?' the dartplayer says, chewing the name over. His own name, he tells you, is Greg. 'Where *is* that?'

'You'll have to ask the taxidriver who brought me.'

'Isn't it what used to be the old Anchor Motel on West End Avenue? Dolly Parton stayed there one time. Least . . .' Willy, disentangling with his tongue a string of mozzarella from his moustache, says '. . . in one of her songs she says she did.'

Greg buys you a Guinness and, after you've drunk it, you buy back. He tells you he doesn't want to work for anyone else in his life again. 'Nossir! I was a graduate from the University of Tennessee. But you don't make money reading books. I'm a blacksmith now,' he tells you. 'I have a good business. My wife's a midwife.'

'That's a good thing for a woman to be,' you say.

'I married a good woman.'

He suggests you and he go have a drink in Brown's.

'What's Brown's?' you ask him.

'It's a bar two blocks from here. You'll like it. It's different. Musicians drink there sometimes.' So you and he and Willy get in his 1969 Pontiac Firebird and drive to Brown's at Blair and 21st. On the way you drop Willy off at his apartment on Southside Avenue and he invites you in for a smoke. Willy lives on the third floor of a three-storey block but he swings his leg up the stairs fine. Willy's wife stops her work at the sewing-machine and kills the sound on the Johnny Carson Show. 'Hi! Nice to meet you. You want a beer?' she says, handing you one anyway. Everything in Willy's apartment is in one room: the TV, the fridge, the bed, the sewing-machine. A window-fan hums. You sit on the bed and have a beer and a smoke while Willy's wife tells you the story of how she won $1000 in a Coke bottle-cap competition way back when it was Old Coke in sexy bottles because she got the one that carried the lucky number. '. . . best moment of my whole life,' she says. 'Up until then.'

'How did you spend the money?' Greg asks her.

'That kind of money spends itself. You might just as well give it away!' she tells him.

'So? Who did you give it away to?'

'His name was Pete Armstrong,' Willy growls. 'A *snake*!'

'He *was* a snake,' Willy's wife says. 'But it was worth it!'
She chuckles. On the TV Johnny Carson is running through
his repertoire of horrible facial expressions, even more
horrible for being without Johnny Carson's voice. 'And
y'know – after we spent the money, about a month after – the
IRS writes me they want the tax on $1000! I couldn't believe
it! I had to go out to *work*!'

Willy's wife has a nice what-the-hell chuckle.

Brown's is an old converted mule-drawn streetcar with
original interior woodwork and slatted benches. The Texas
Rangers are playing the Cleveland All Stars on the TV. The
pitcher for the Rangers, apparently, has just sent the All Stars
back to the benches with a No Hitter. The bar is going wild.
The barman is trying to watch the replay over his shoulder
while he serves the beer. An Alfred Hitchcock blonde called
Sally joins you – she's a little drunk – and, a moment later,
Graham, corpulent, unshaven, a bit jet-lagged. He's smoking
John Player's Silk Cut, King Size. The conversation careers
from here to there. You and Greg are high on Willy's wife's
grass so you hardly notice.

Sally, speaking chiefly to Greg, says: 'Me and Marty just
came back this afternoon from one wild drunk Louisville
weekend!' She's dressed in a slim double-breasted grey suit –
the kind that Lois, Perry Mason's secretary, used to wear.

Graham plays bass in a band. He's telling you about the
tour he just got back from today. '. . . so we were playing in a
pub in North Humber Land – just a pub gig, right? – and the
audience was all got up in cowboy outfits! You hear me?
Silver spurs! Tooled-leather holsters! Stetsons! When, right
in the middle of the set, these crazy guys start firing their
fucking pistols into the air! Me, I dived for cover! Jesus! I'm
telling you, man, I was *scared*! Then, after the gig, this
Englishman comes up to me – dressed like one of the James
brothers – and says: "Hey! You guys aren't a f'real Country
band *are* you?" I thought he was going to *shoot* me! No we
aren't, I tell him. But you're not a f'real fucking cowboy
either!'

'They have this bar in Louisville with every drink in the

world and they write your name up or something if you drink them all,' Sally is telling Greg. 'So we got these two guys to looks us over and then buy us drinks.' It all comes out in a rush and you realize she's coked up. 'They just couldn't work us out, whether we were hookers or what! . . .' She's wearing pink lipstick – of a shade of pink only a lipstick-manufacturer would have a name for. You realize you're staring at her lips. 'Okay . . . so where's the Party?' they go.

'Party?' Greg says.

'Sure. Let's collect Marty and find us a party. Hey, that rhymes!'

Greg begins to apply the handbrake but Sally is too drunk or coked up to notice. 'We'll be heading back to The Tavern soon,' he tells her.

'You going to The Tavern right now?' She looks at you for the first time, smiling, as if it's up to you.

'Well . . .' You look towards Greg. '. . . soon, I guess.'

'I'll see you boys there!' she informs you. 'I have my car. You coming Graham?'

'Me, I'm too wiped out,' Graham tells her.

Greg drives you back to The Tavern in the Firebird. He's quiet, smoking one of Graham's Silk Cut. You're both quiet.

'What's with Willy's leg?' you ask him. Sideways, without taking his eyes off the road or the cigarette out of his mouth, he tells you:

'Nam!'

In The Tavern Greg says something to the girl behind the bar and, to you: 'Look, I got to be getting home. 's been nice talking to you.' You shake hands and he leaves immediately. He leaves so quickly you wonder whether he took offence on account of your asking about Willy's leg. The taxidriver with the circus liontamer's moustache, you notice, is over in the nook playing the ancient Miss America pinball table, concentrating on nudging the table ever so lightly with his circus strongman's arms: Bambam! Bambam! On the TV the leather-padded umpire is crouching behind the plate, the pitcher for the Rangers looking round before coming out of his wind, the hitter shaping up for the strike.

150

'How did you like Brown's?' the barkeep says while she pours from the Old Grandad bottle into an ice-filled tumbler.

'I liked it,' you tell her. 'It's, ah, different.'

'It's different, yeah!' she agrees. 'Musicians drink there sometimes.'

'So Greg told me.'

'He did? Well, everything in Nashville has to happen to you twice.'

You look at her. She's about twenty. 'Does it?' you say.

'Oh sure! And like the song says, it's always a lot better second time round.'

How can she know so much and be so young? you wonder.

'Stick 'em up!' A finger digs you in the back. 'You better make that two! Or I'll blow you to Chattanooga!'

You look up over your shoulder at a pair of pink lips and your heart starts going like a gong. Because, in an instant, you understand everything. Everything that has happened and everything that will happen. You say howdy but the woman with pink lips is not particularly looking your way. Her eyes are scanning the bar for a guy wearing Duck Head bib overalls.

'So where's Greg Hanson?'

'Ah . . . He had to go. Home.'

'*Home*! Well . . .' She hesitates, wrinkles her nose, – 'The skunk!' – climbs onto the stool, has to hike up her skirt to get on it, sighs – 'The skunk!' – opens her purse, pays for the drinks. The shoulders of her 2B pencil grey suit coat are padded. They would look severe except that her yellow hair is straggling down in places where it has come loose from its grips. Under her open suit coat she has on a peaches and cream skin-coloured crêpe blouse, unbuttoned at the neck. Perry Mason's secretary, Lois, never looked like this.

You can't work her out. You're no different than the fellers in Louisville.

Sally plays with her glass of bourbon. She has pink cuticleless nails. She taps the side of the glass with one of them. 'That's the way my luck runs with men. They take off when they see me come. I'm sorry. Did you tell me your name?' She turns, looks at you, smiles. Everything happens to you twice in Nashville. The second time, the song says, is always better. 'I'm a thousand miles out of my mind. You can

151

probably tell. It's always the same. Some people are born to be tied down, some to tie people down. I wish I knew which I am. Fact is there's no help for it, when a man marries the wrong woman. What can you do? I guess he always does. I know I did. They go wrong as soon as you marry them. Why am I talking like this? Why does whisky make me lose my head? Got me sitting in a bar with you when I should be home in bed. Hey! You know something? That rhymes!'